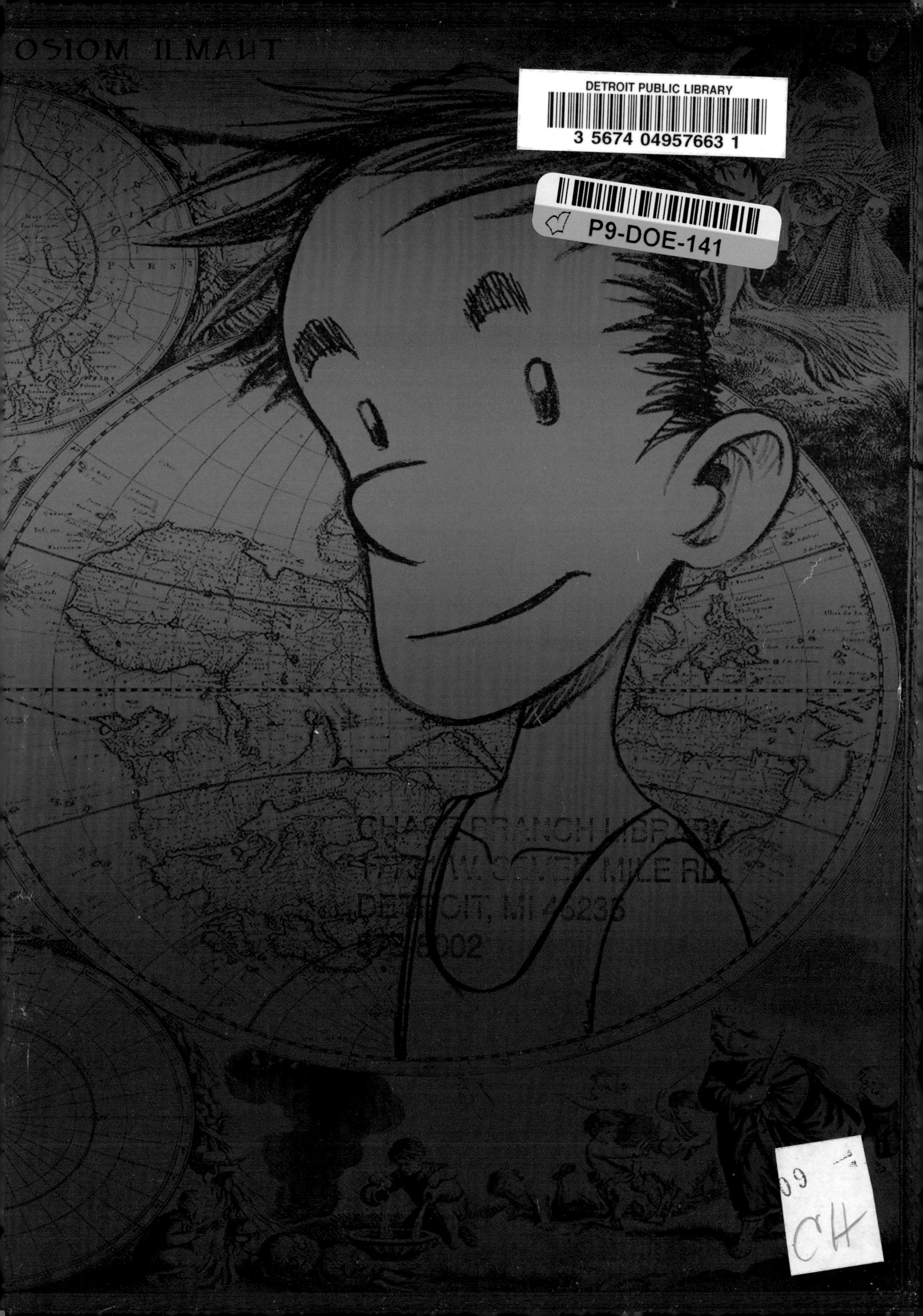

the ElseWheRe CHRONICLES

BOOK THREE
THE MASTER OF SHADOWS

ART
BANNISTER

STORY
NYKKO

COLORS
JAFFRÉ

GRAPHIC UNIVERSE™ • MINNEAPOLIS • NEW YORK

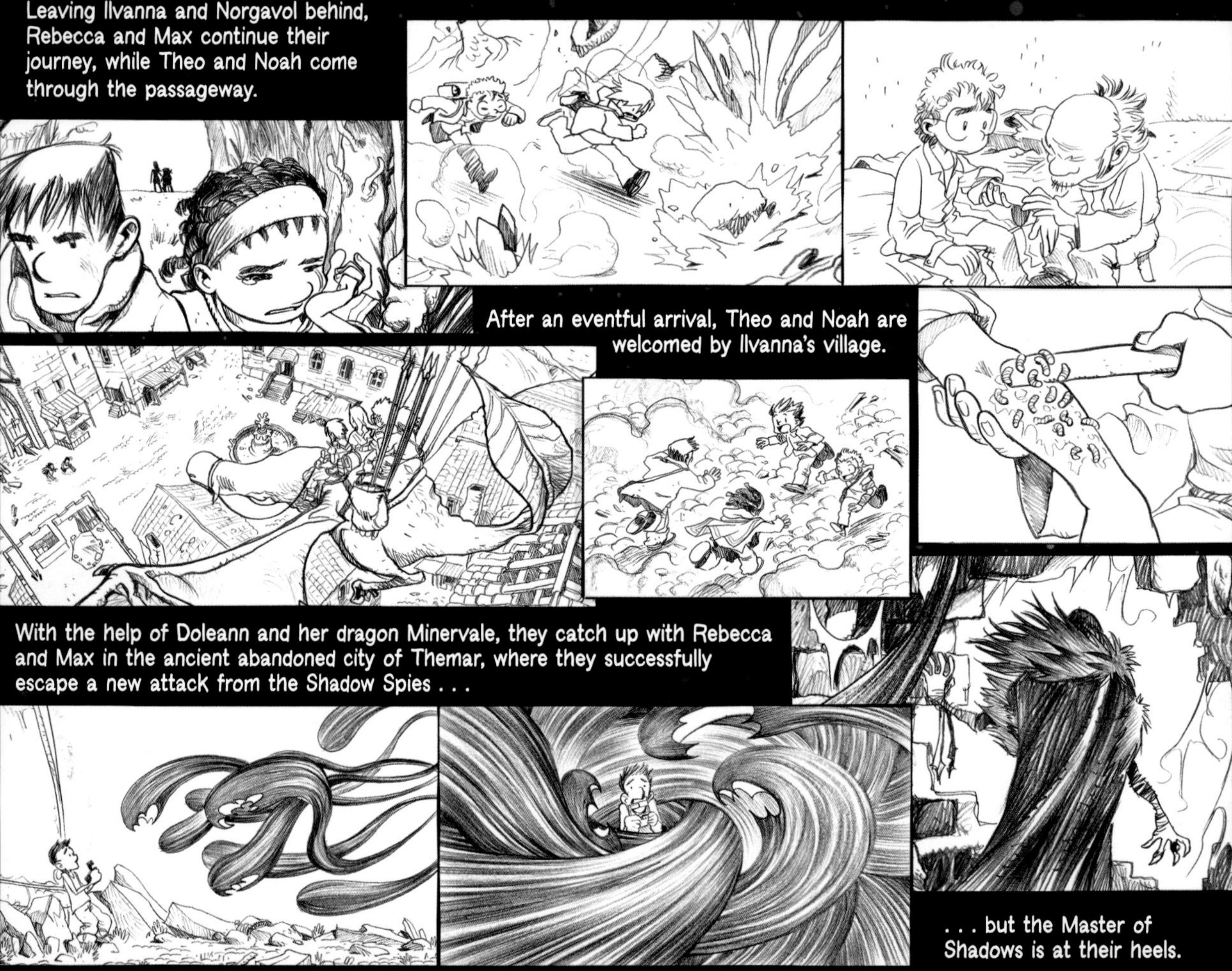
Leaving Ilvanna and Norgavol behind, Rebecca and Max continue their journey, while Theo and Noah come through the passageway.
After an eventful arrival, Theo and Noah are welcomed by Ilvanna's village.
With the help of Doleann and her dragon Minervale, they catch up with Rebecca and Max in the ancient abandoned city of Themar, where they successfully escape a new attack from the Shadow Spies . . .
. . . but the Master of Shadows is at their heels.

Nykko and Corentin, bravo for toughing it out this far.

Flora, thank you for supporting us from day to day but most of all for the cakes.

—Bannister

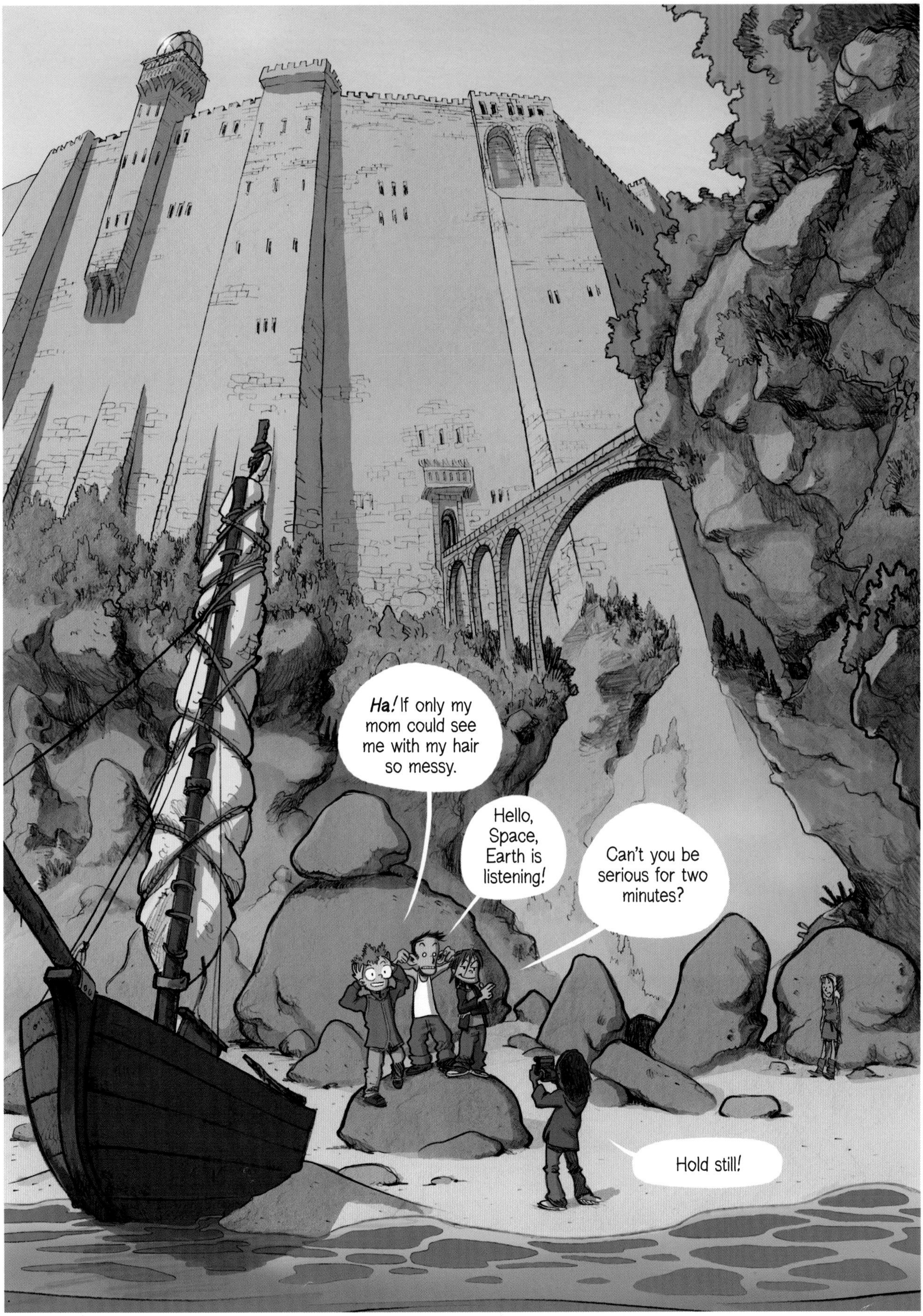
Ha! If only my mom could see me with my hair so messy.
Hello, Space, Earth is listening!
Can't you be serious for two minutes?
Hold still!

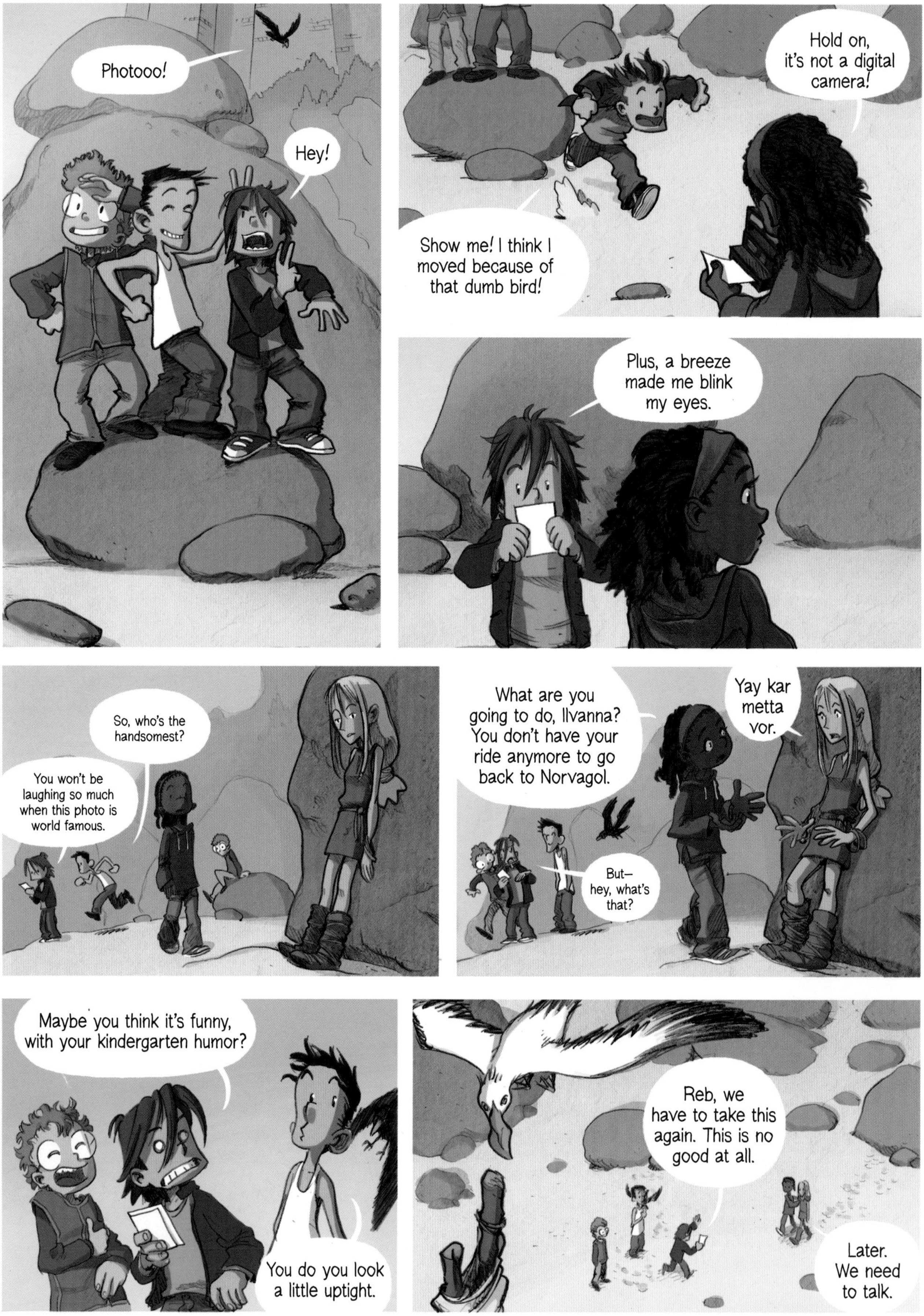

Photooo!
Hey!
Hold on, it's not a digital camera!
Show me! I think I moved because of that dumb bird!
Plus, a breeze made me blink my eyes.
So, who's the handsomest?
You won't be laughing so much when this photo is world famous.
What are you going to do, Ilvanna? You don't have your ride anymore to go back to Norvagol.
Yay kar metta vor.
But— hey, what's that?
Maybe you think it's funny, with your kindergarten humor?
You do you look a little uptight.
Reb, we have to take this again. This is no good at all.
Later. We need to talk.

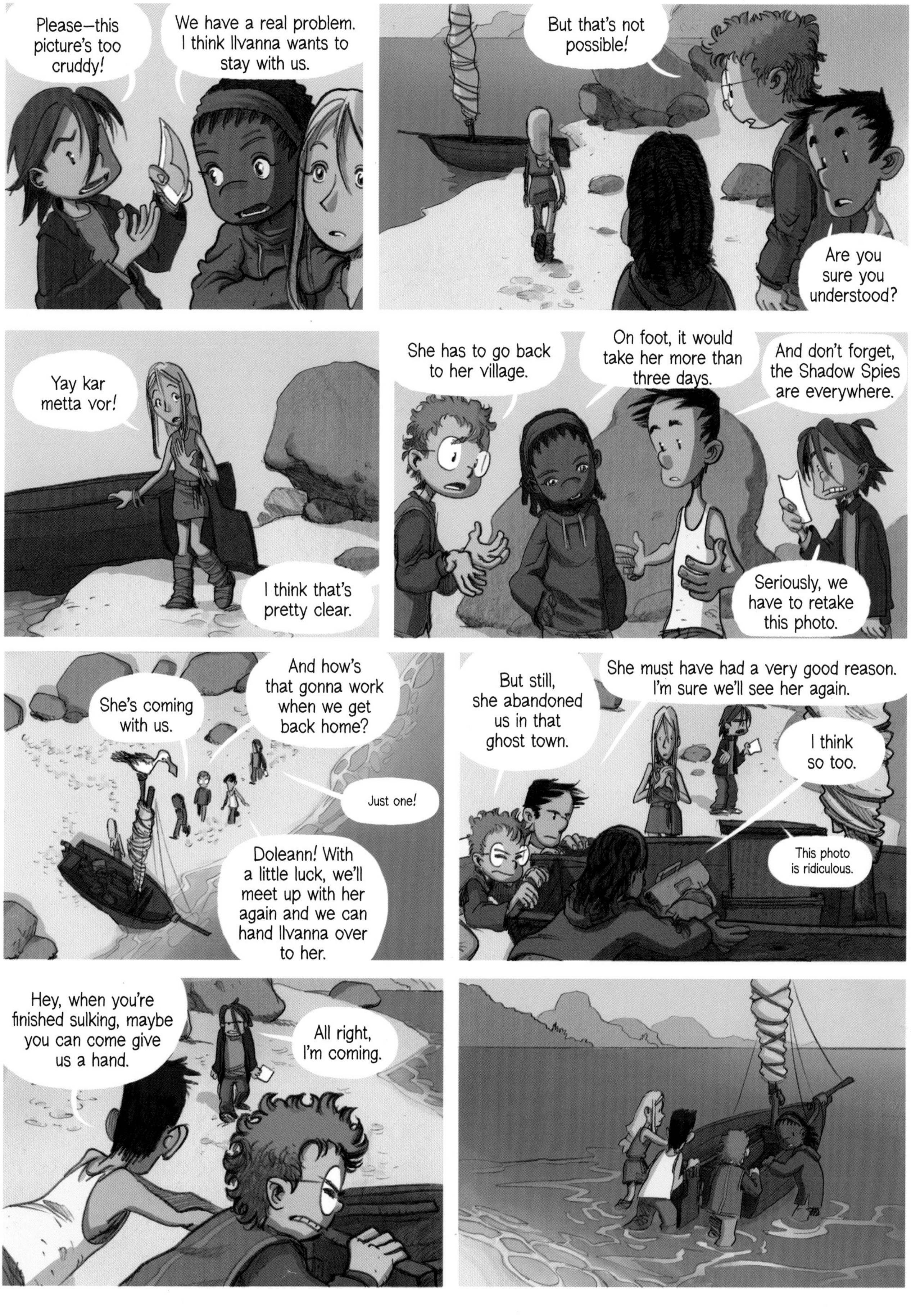
Please—this picture's too cruddy!
We have a real problem. I think Ilvanna wants to stay with us.
But that's not possible!
Are you sure you understood?
Yay kar metta vor!
I think that's pretty clear.
She has to go back to her village.
On foot, it would take her more than three days.
And don't forget, the Shadow Spies are everywhere.
Seriously, we have to retake this photo.
She's coming with us.
And how's that gonna work when we get back home?
Just one!
Doleann! With a little luck, we'll meet up with her again and we can hand Ilvanna over to her.
But still, she abandoned us in that ghost town.
She must have had a very good reason. I'm sure we'll see her again.
I think so too.
This photo is ridiculous.
Hey, when you're finished sulking, maybe you can come give us a hand.
All right, I'm coming.

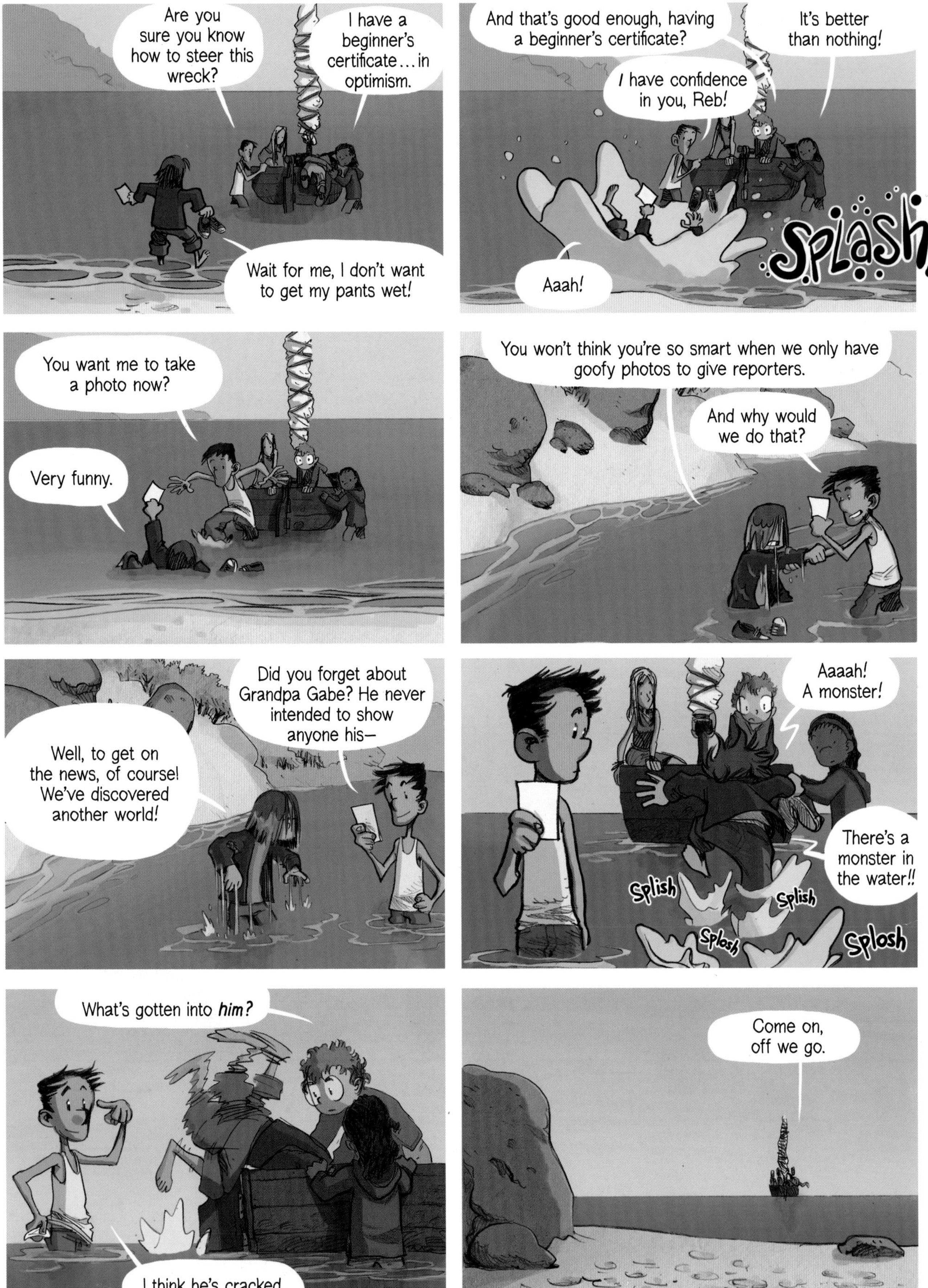
Are you sure you know how to steer this wreck?
I have a beginner's certificate... in optimism.
Wait for me, I don't want to get my pants wet!
And that's good enough, having a beginner's certificate?
It's better than nothing!
I have confidence in you, Reb!
SPLASH!
Aaah!
You want me to take a photo now?
Very funny.
You won't think you're so smart when we only have goofy photos to give reporters.
And why would we do that?
Did you forget about Grandpa Gabe? He never intended to show anyone his–
Well, to get on the news, of course! We've discovered another world!
Aaaah! A monster!
There's a monster in the water!!
Splish
Splish
Splosh
Splosh
What's gotten into ***him?***
I think he's cracked.
Come on, off we go.

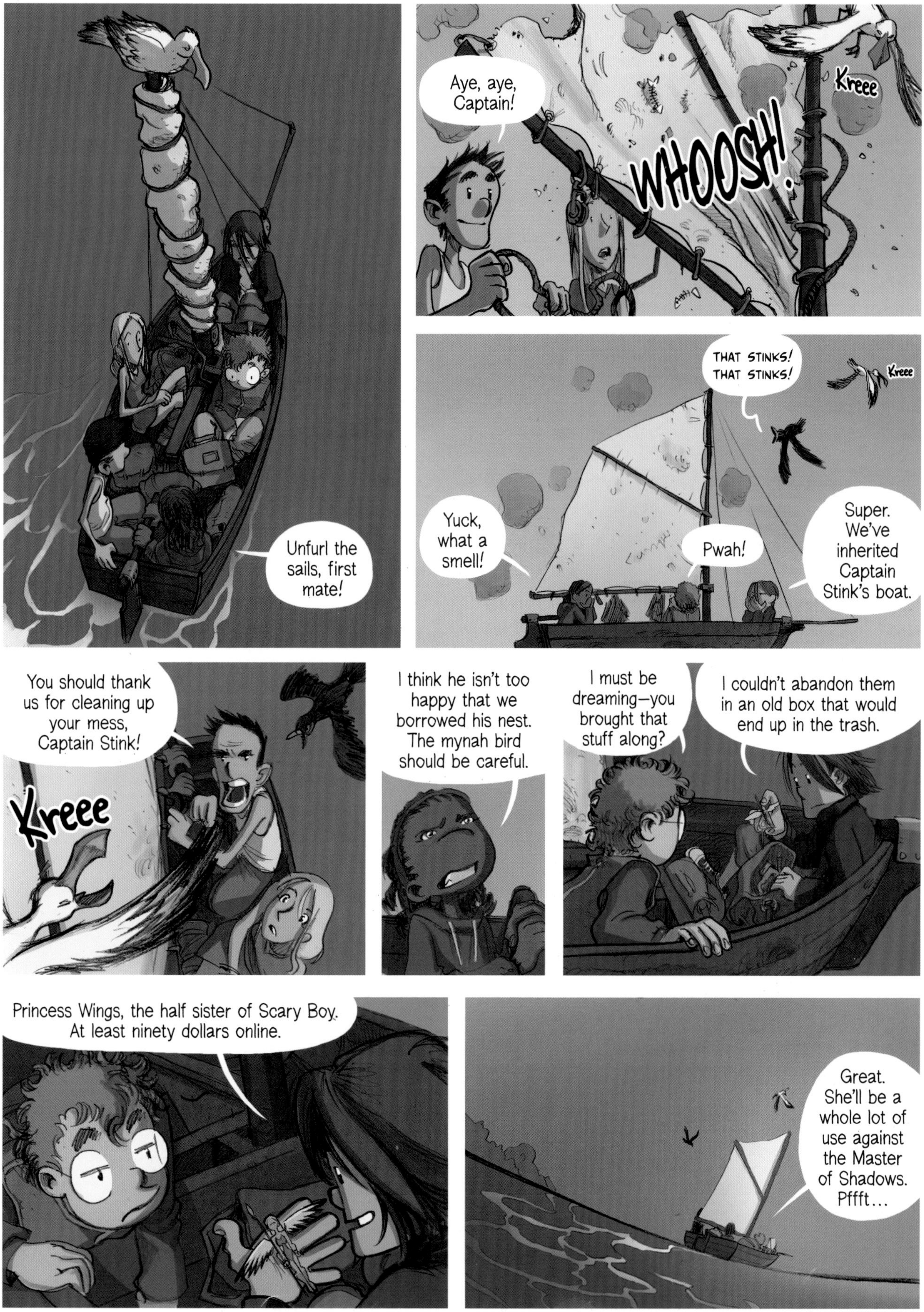
Unfurl the sails, first mate!
Aye, aye, Captain!
Kreee
WHOOSH!
THAT STINKS! THAT STINKS!
Kreee
Yuck, what a smell!
Pwah!
Super. We've inherited Captain Stink's boat.
You should thank us for cleaning up your mess, Captain Stink!
Kreee
I think he isn't too happy that we borrowed his nest. The mynah bird should be careful.
I must be dreaming—you brought that stuff along?
I couldn't abandon them in an old box that would end up in the trash.
Princess Wings, the half sister of Scary Boy. At least ninety dollars online.
Great. She'll be a whole lot of use against the Master of Shadows. Pffft...

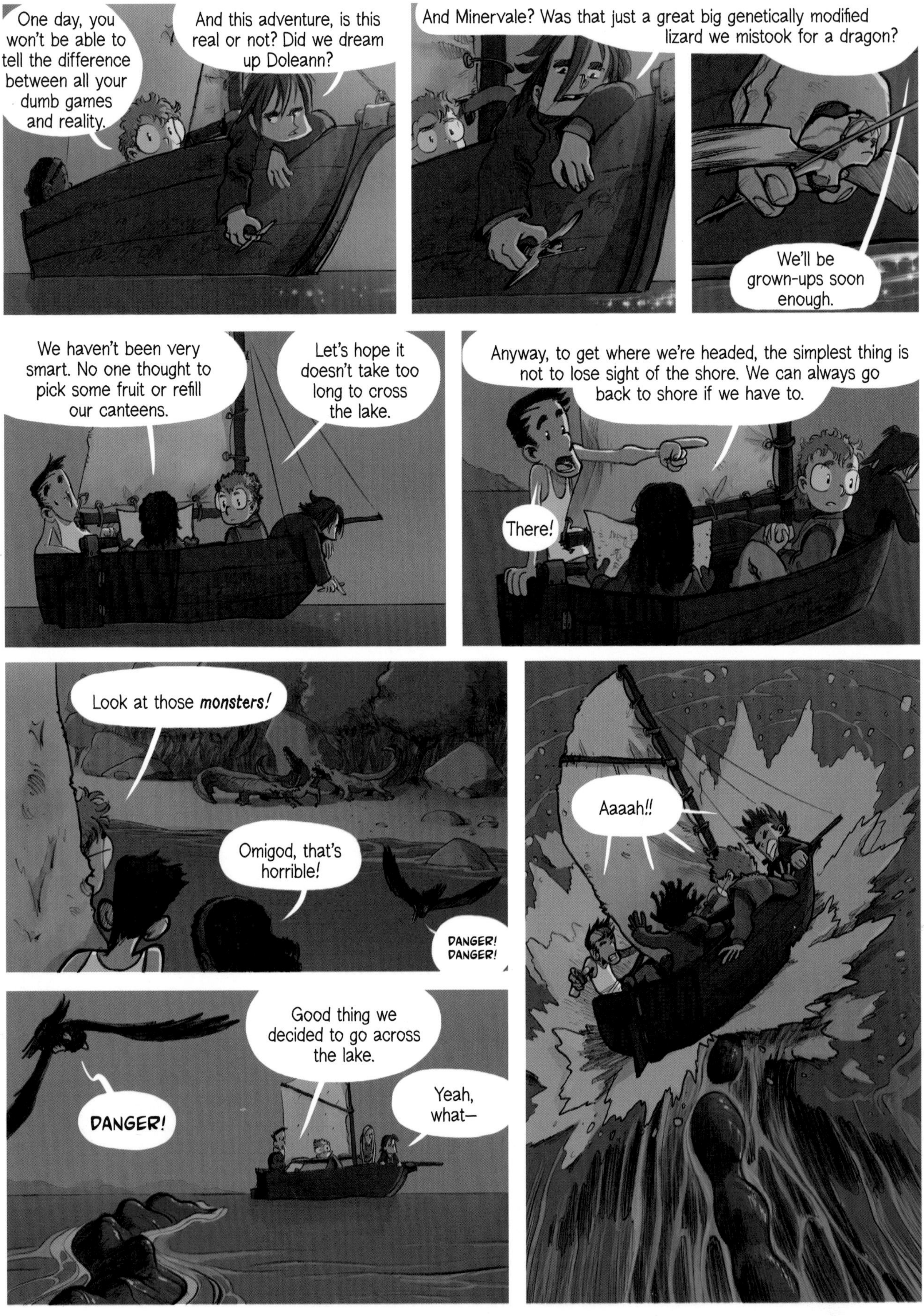
One day, you won't be able to tell the difference between all your dumb games and reality.
And this adventure, is this real or not? Did we dream up Doleann?
And Minervale? Was that just a great big genetically modified lizard we mistook for a dragon?
We'll be grown-ups soon enough.
We haven't been very smart. No one thought to pick some fruit or refill our canteens.
Let's hope it doesn't take too long to cross the lake.
Anyway, to get where we're headed, the simplest thing is not to lose sight of the shore. We can always go back to shore if we have to.
There!
Look at those *monsters!*
Omigod, that's horrible!
DANGER! DANGER!
Good thing we decided to go across the lake.
Yeah, what—
DANGER!
Aaaah!!

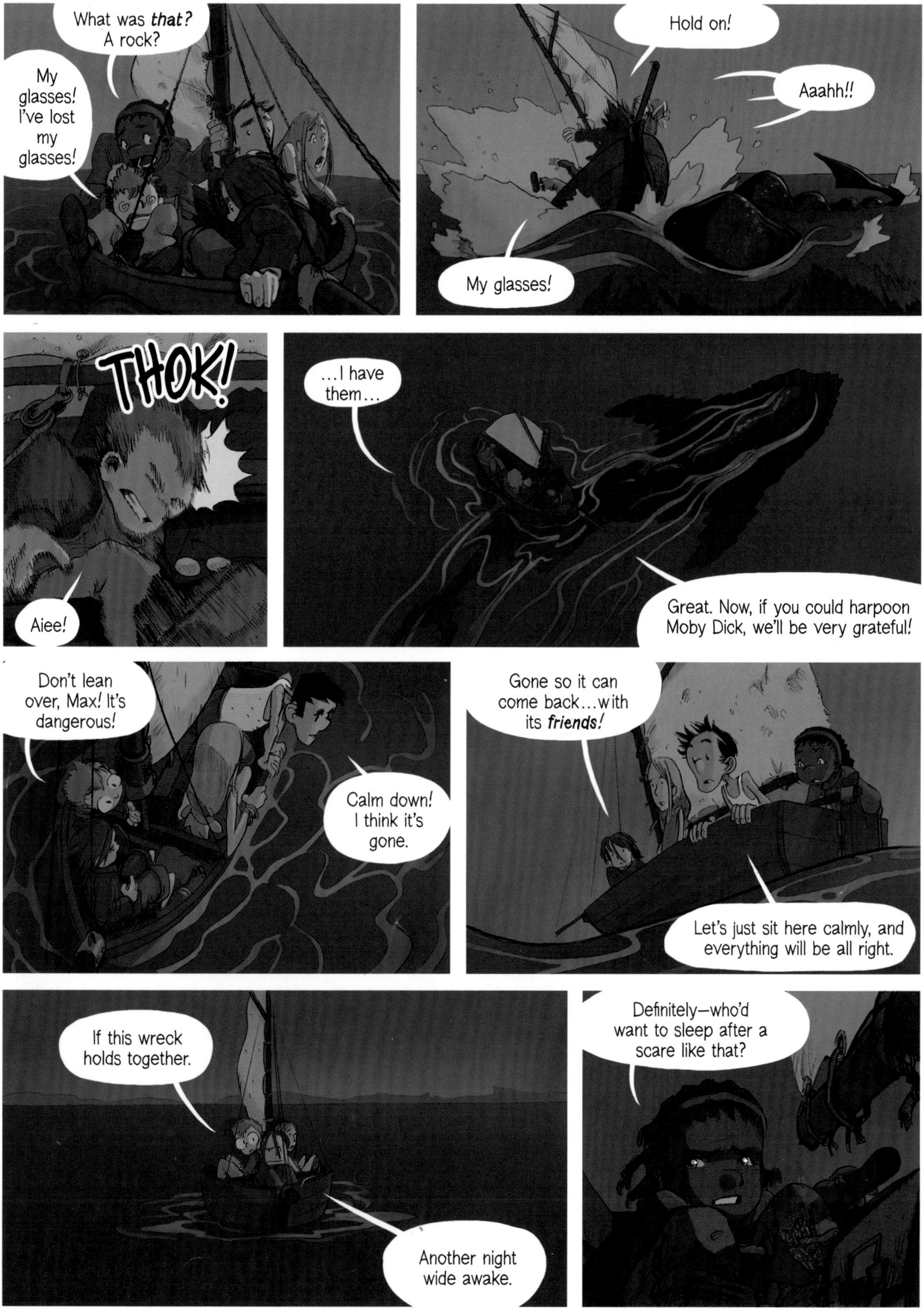
What was **that?** A rock?
My glasses! I've lost my glasses!
Hold on!
Aaahh!!
My glasses!
THOK!
Aiee!
...I have them...
Great. Now, if you could harpoon Moby Dick, we'll be very grateful!
Don't lean over, Max! It's dangerous!
Calm down! I think it's gone.
Gone so it can come back...with its **friends!**
Let's just sit here calmly, and everything will be all right.
If this wreck holds together.
Another night wide awake.
Definitely—who'd want to sleep after a scare like that?

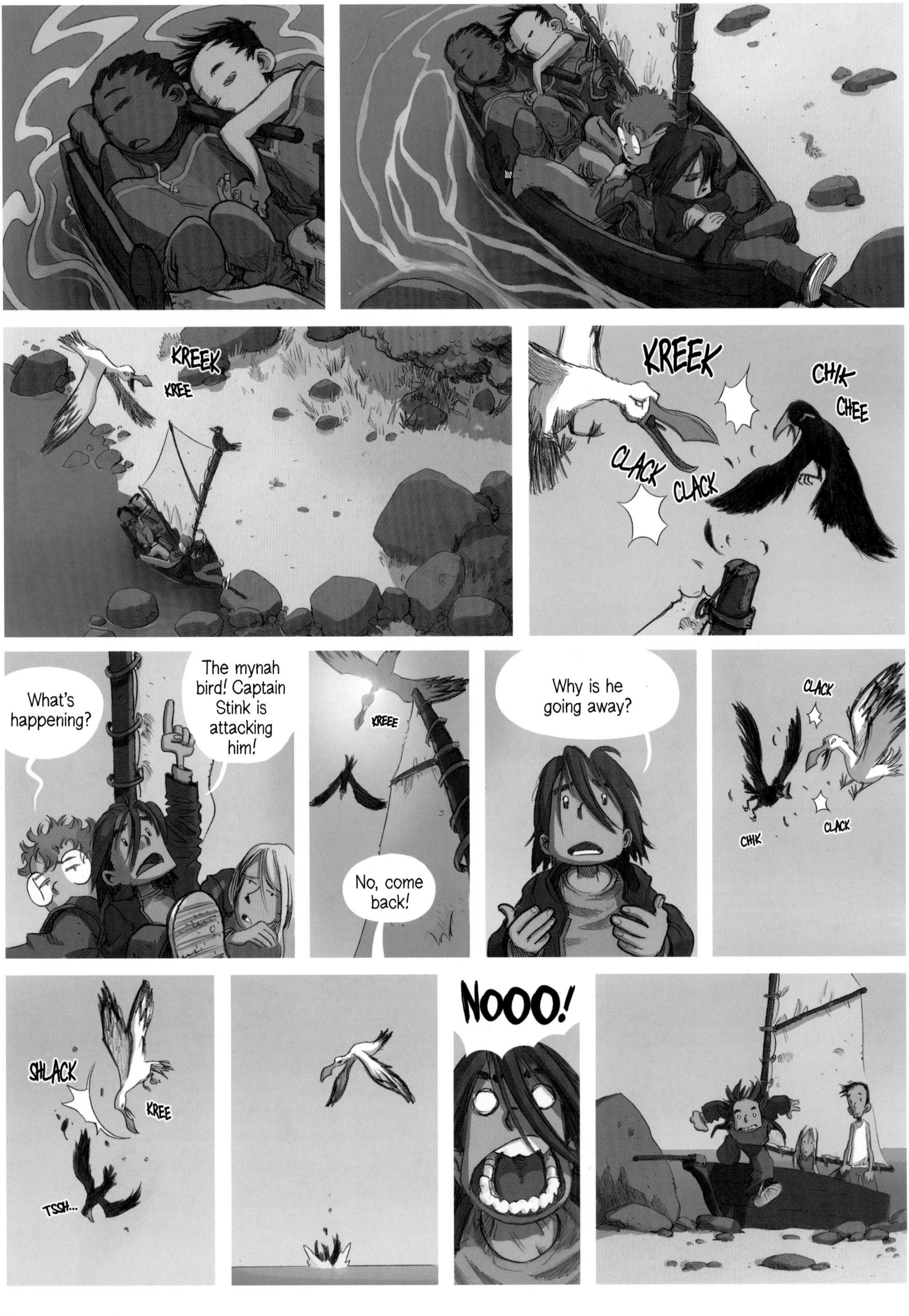
KREEK
KREE
KREEK
CHIK
CHEE
CLACK
CLACK
What's happening?
The mynah bird! Captain Stink is attacking him!
KREEE
No, come back!
Why is he going away?
CLACK
CLACK
CHIK
SHLACK
KREE
TSSH...
NOOO!

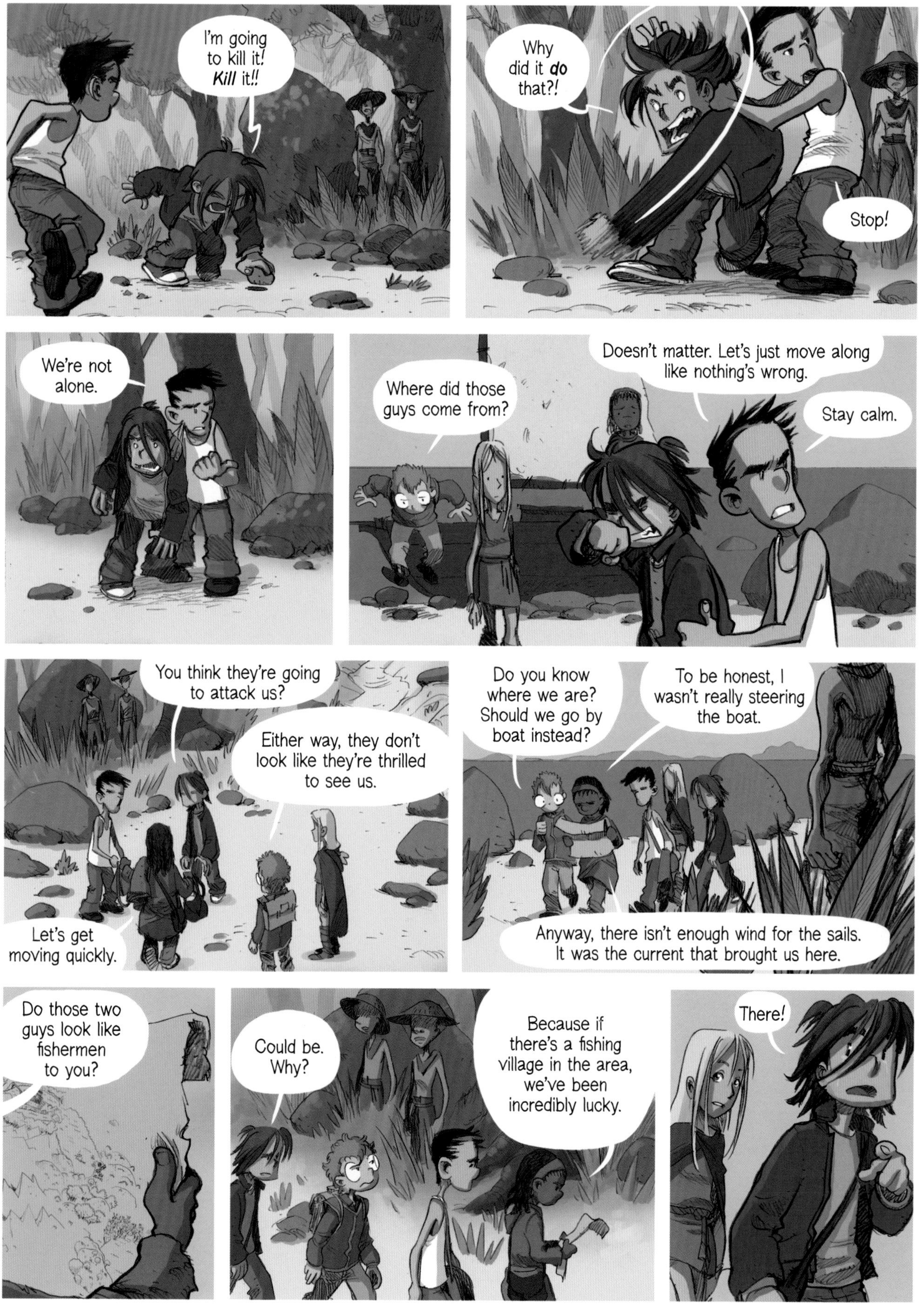
I'm going to kill it! *Kill* it!!
Why did it *do* that?!
Stop!
We're not alone.
Where did those guys come from?
Doesn't matter. Let's just move along like nothing's wrong.
Stay calm.
You think they're going to attack us?
Either way, they don't look like they're thrilled to see us.
Let's get moving quickly.
Do you know where we are? Should we go by boat instead?
To be honest, I wasn't really steering the boat.
Anyway, there isn't enough wind for the sails. It was the current that brought us here.
Do those two guys look like fishermen to you?
Could be. Why?
Because if there's a fishing village in the area, we've been incredibly lucky.
There!

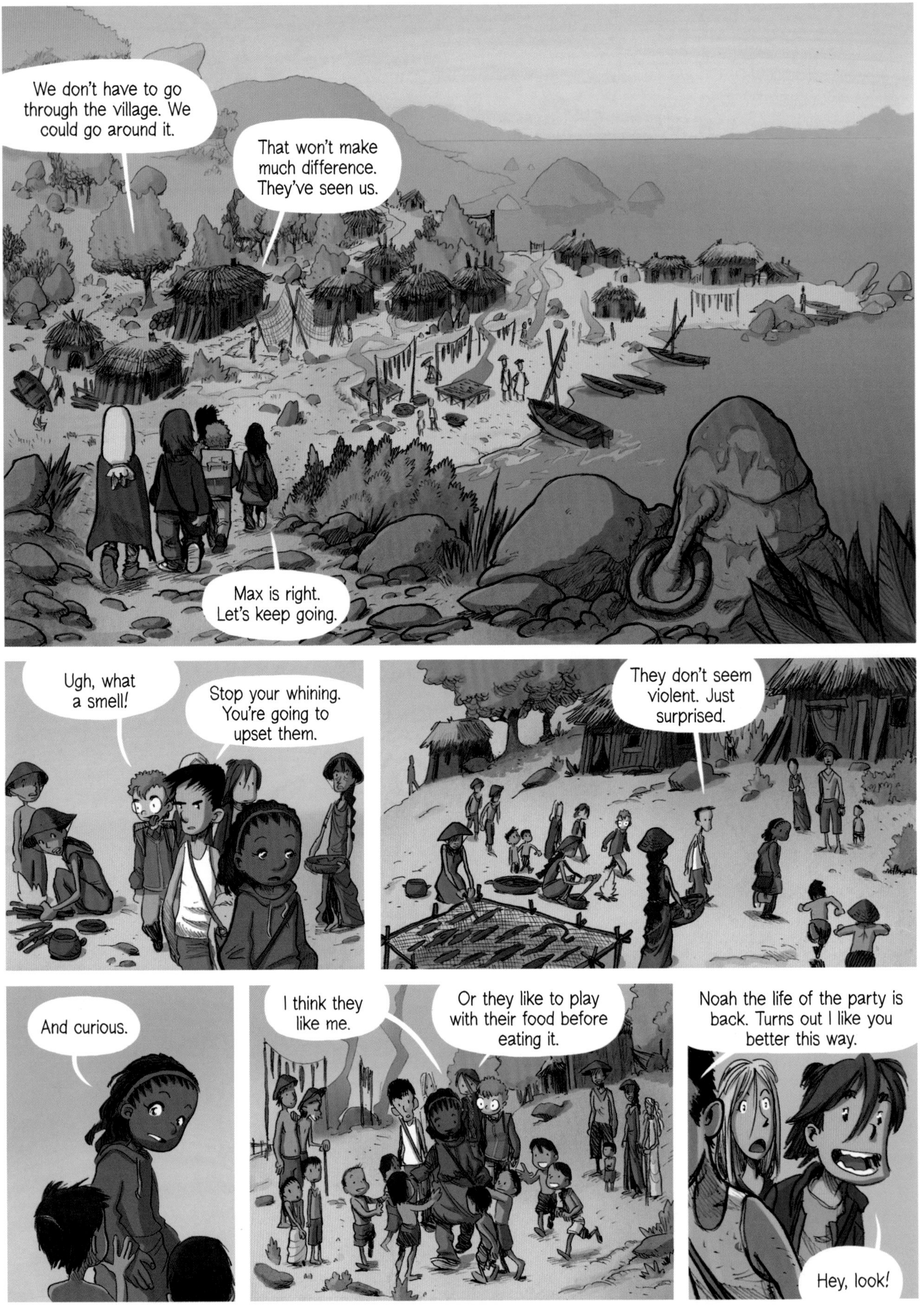
We don't have to go through the village. We could go around it.
That won't make much difference. They've seen us.
Max is right. Let's keep going.
Ugh, what a smell!
Stop your whining. You're going to upset them.
They don't seem violent. Just surprised.
And curious.
I think they like me.
Or they like to play with their food before eating it.
Noah the life of the party is back. Turns out I like you better this way.
Hey, look!

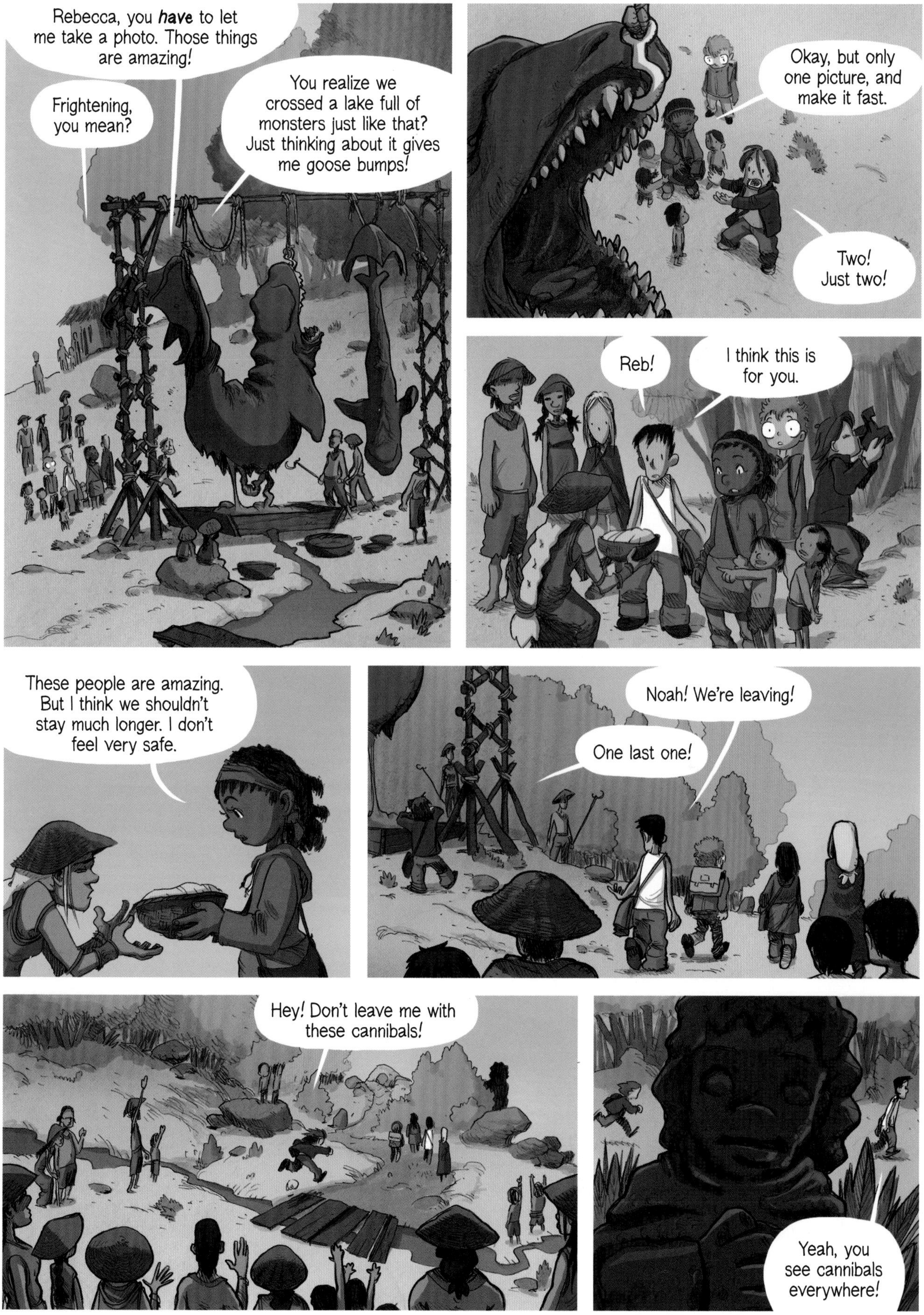
Rebecca, you *have* to let me take a photo. Those things are amazing!
Frightening, you mean?
You realize we crossed a lake full of monsters just like that? Just thinking about it gives me goose bumps!
Okay, but only one picture, and make it fast.
Two! Just two!
Reb!
I think this is for you.
These people are amazing. But I think we shouldn't stay much longer. I don't feel very safe.
Noah! We're leaving!
One last one!
Hey! Don't leave me with these cannibals!
Yeah, you see cannibals everywhere!

They're not following us.

Good. What's in the basket?

Dried fish.

Ugh, lucky us.

Great—we need to eat. But we should think about refilling our canteens.

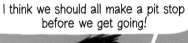

We could pick fruit!

But which ones? How do we know these are edible?

Sorry, but I've gotta go, right now!

I think we should all make a pit stop before we get going!

That's the main reason why I hate camping out in the wild.

Didn't you learn how to dig a ditch for a latrine from the Cub Scout manual?

Let's not go too far, and everyone meet here again in ten minutes tops.

I don't have a watch!

Unless you're constipated, ten minutes is more than enough. Hehehe.

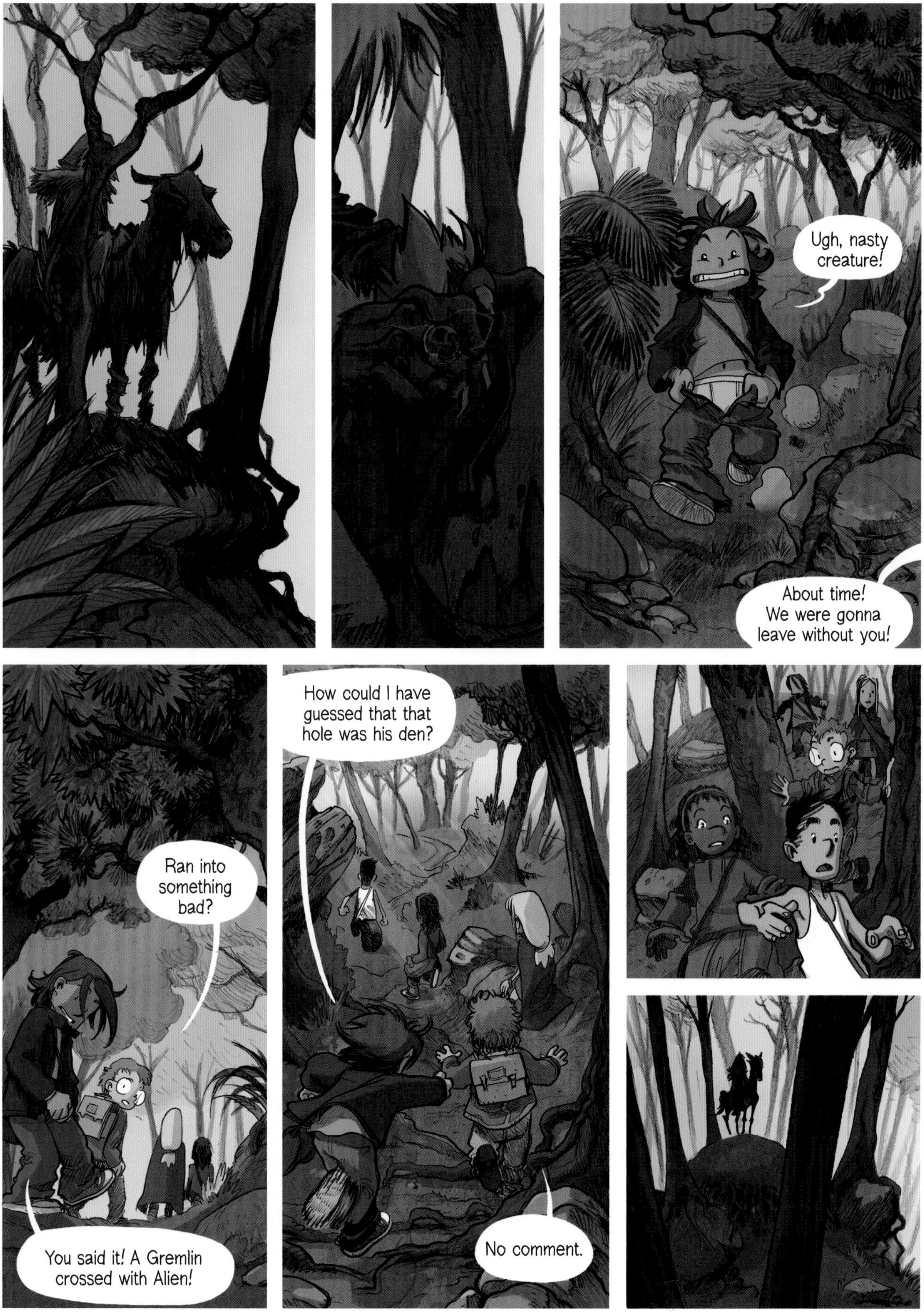
Ugh, nasty creature!
About time! We were gonna leave without you!
Ran into something bad?
You said it! A Gremlin crossed with Alien!
How could I have guessed that that hole was his den?
No comment.

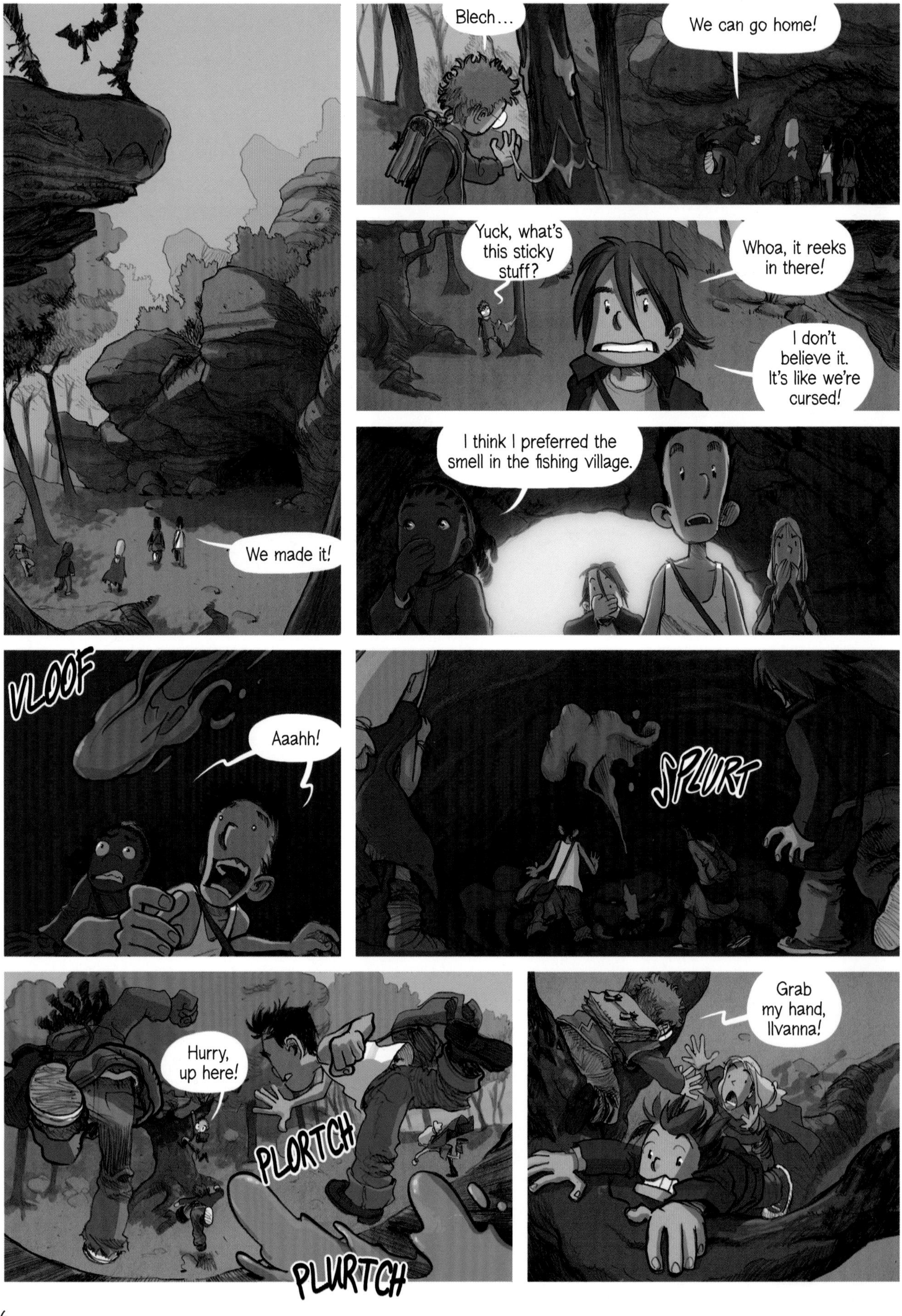
We made it!
Blech...
We can go home!
Yuck, what's this sticky stuff?
Whoa, it reeks in there!
I don't believe it. It's like we're cursed!
I think I preferred the smell in the fishing village.
VLOOF
Aaahh!
SPLURT
Hurry, up here!
PLORTCH
PLURTCH
Grab my hand, Ilvanna!

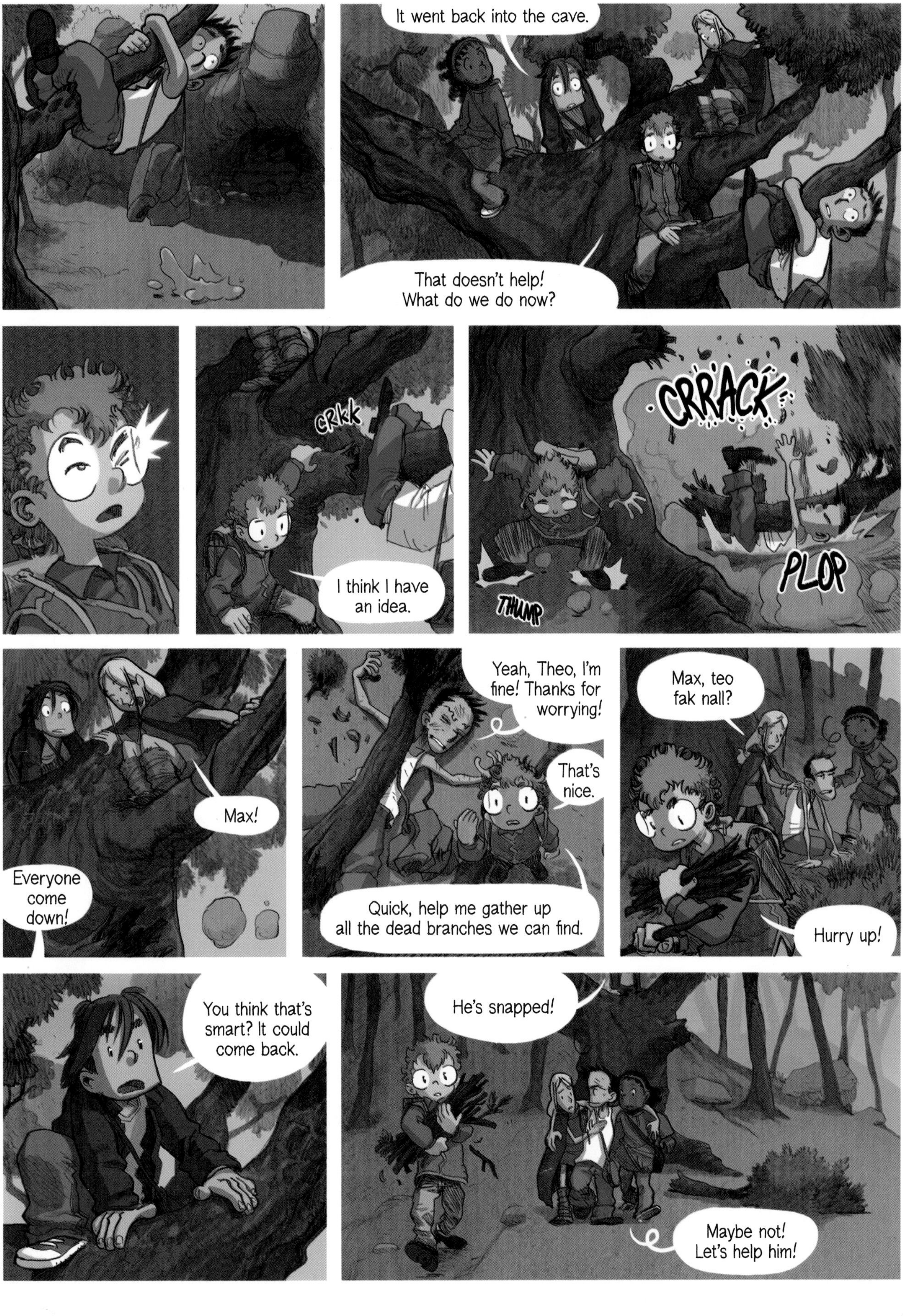

It went back into the cave.
That doesn't help! What do we do now?
CRKK
I think I have an idea.
CRRACK
THUMP
PLOP
Max!
Everyone come down!
Yeah, Theo, I'm fine! Thanks for worrying!
That's nice.
Quick, help me gather up all the dead branches we can find.
Max, teo fak nall?
Hurry up!
You think that's smart? It could come back.
He's snapped!
Maybe not! Let's help him!

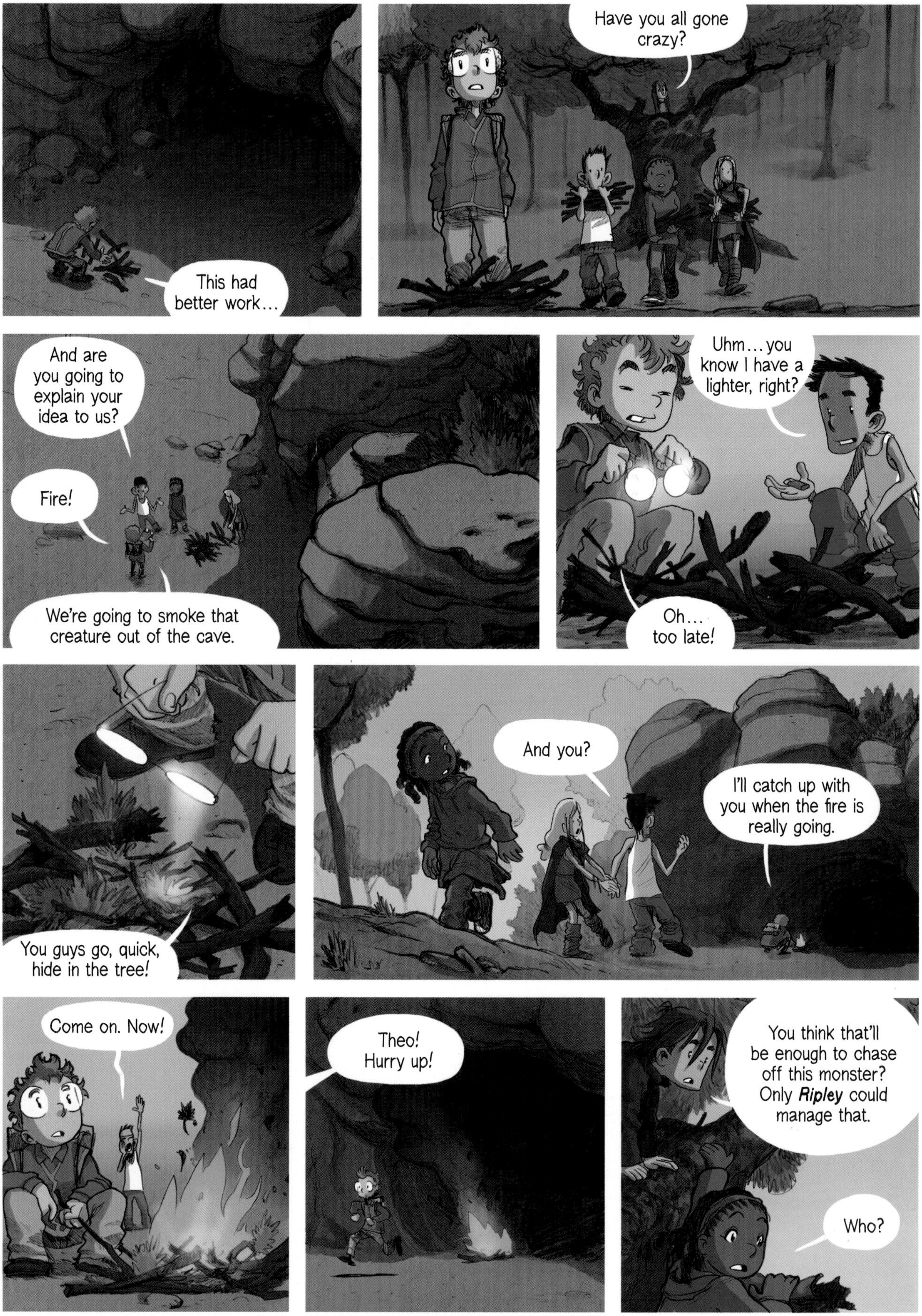
This had better work...
Have you all gone crazy?
And are you going to explain your idea to us?
Fire!
We're going to smoke that creature out of the cave.
Uhm... you know I have a lighter, right?
Oh... too late!
You guys go, quick, hide in the tree!
And you?
I'll catch up with you when the fire is really going.
Come on. Now!
Theo! Hurry up!
You think that'll be enough to chase off this monster? Only *Ripley* could manage that.
Who?

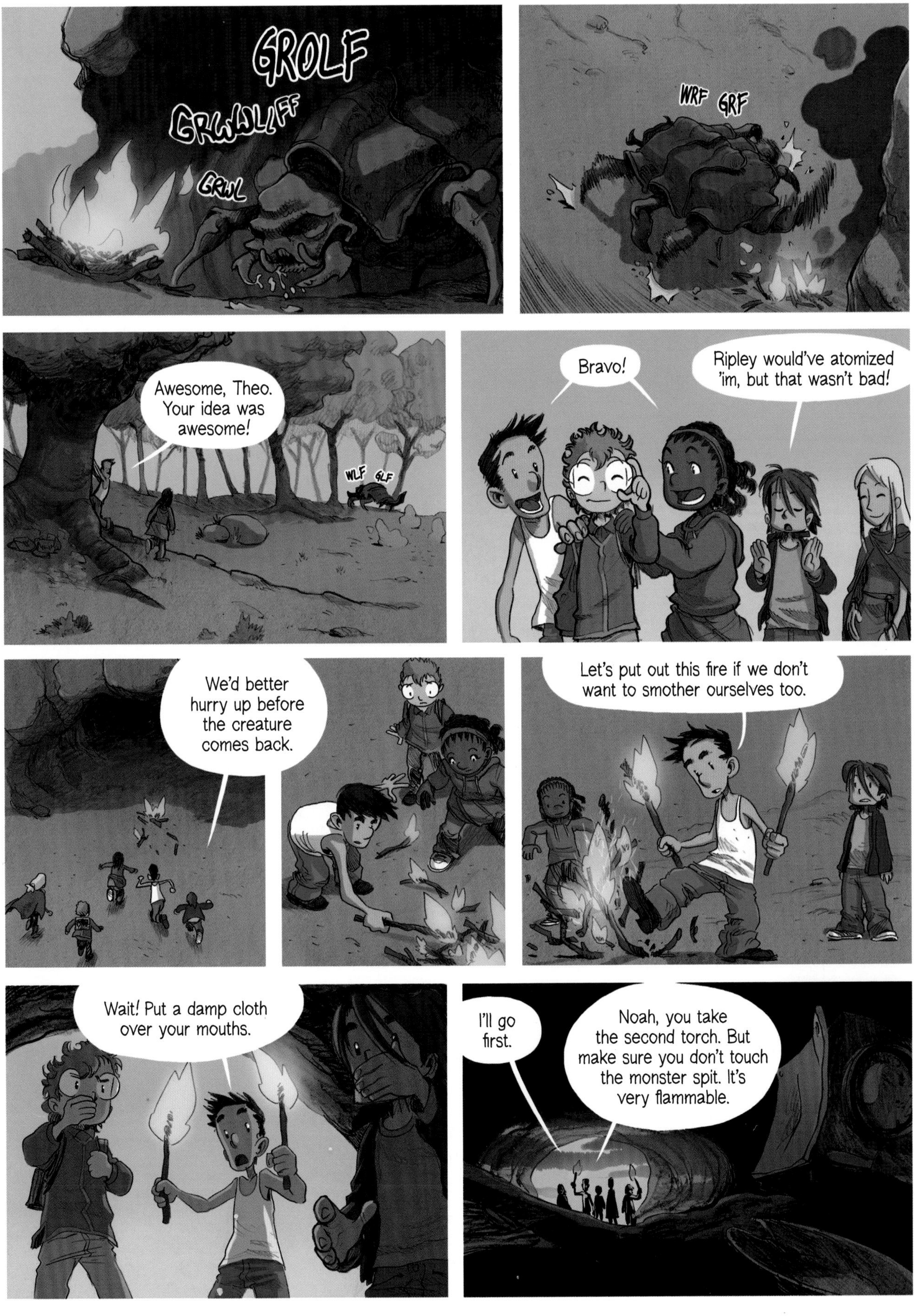
GROLF
GRWWLLIFF
GRWL
WRF GRF
Awesome, Theo. Your idea was awesome!
WLF GLF
Bravo!
Ripley would've atomized 'im, but that wasn't bad!
We'd better hurry up before the creature comes back.
Let's put out this fire if we don't want to smother ourselves too.
Wait! Put a damp cloth over your mouths.
I'll go first.
Noah, you take the second torch. But make sure you don't touch the monster spit. It's very flammable.

If you find the creature's eggs, definitely don't lean over them.

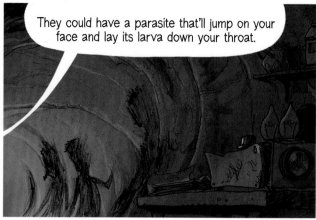

They could have a parasite that'll jump on your face and lay its larva down your throat.

Noah?

What?

Shut up!

Oh no! The monster's destroyed our last chance. We'll be trapped here forever.

Listen to this! "It is hunting me and is bound to discover where I am hiding.

I am the cause of a tragedy and I cannot, now, refuse to accept the terrifying consequences.

I am going to disappear. But first, because I cannot correct my mistakes, I must destroy the passageways.

May the fifth eye unite our two worlds." And it's signed, Gabriel Delille.

Let's take everything we can use and go back to Ilvanna's village…

Wait!

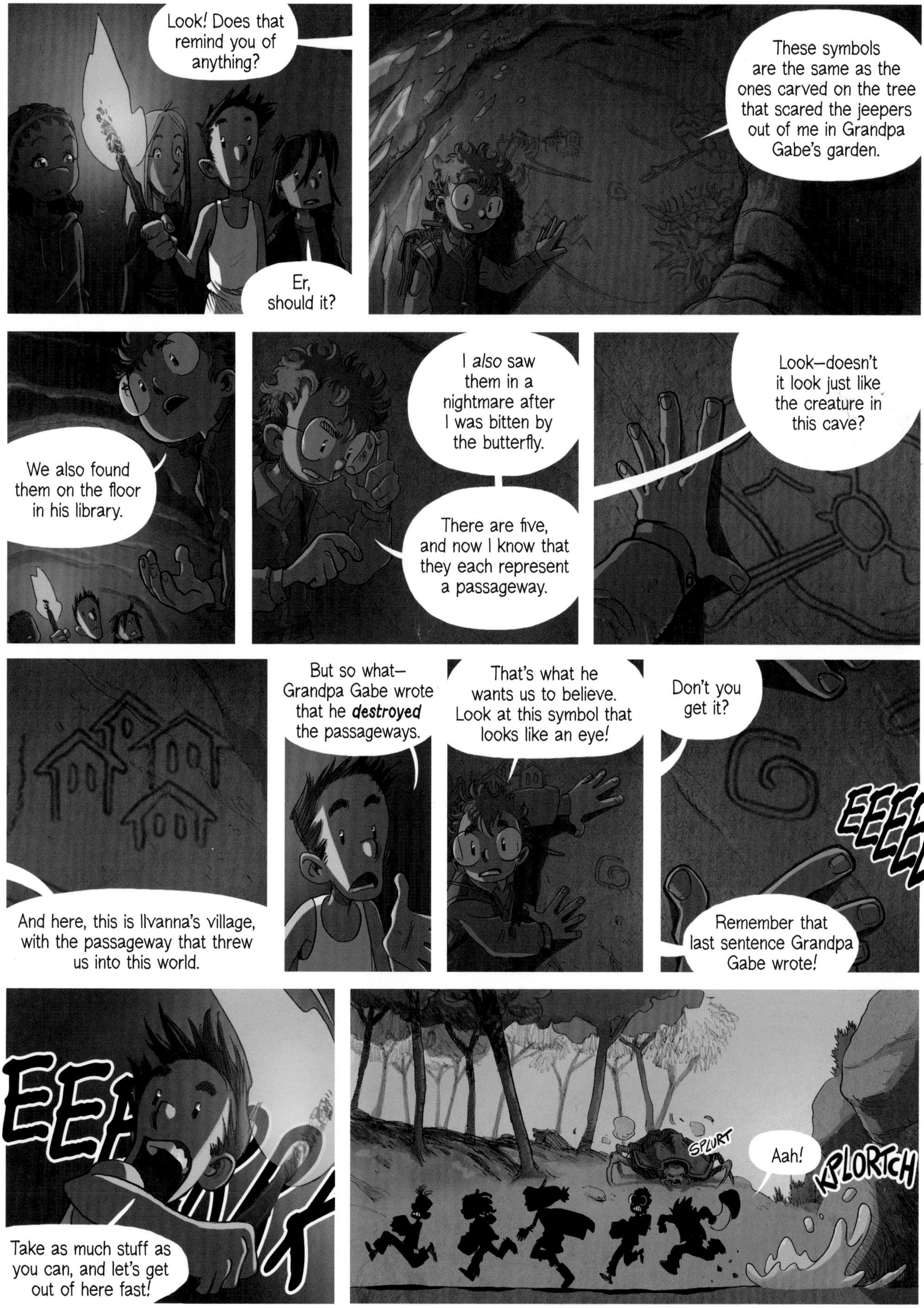

Look! Does that remind you of anything?
Er, should it?
These symbols are the same as the ones carved on the tree that scared the jeepers out of me in Grandpa Gabe's garden.
We also found them on the floor in his library.
I also saw them in a nightmare after I was bitten by the butterfly.
There are five, and now I know that they each represent a passageway.
Look—doesn't it look just like the creature in this cave?
And here, this is Ilvanna's village, with the passageway that threw us into this world.
But so what—Grandpa Gabe wrote that he destroyed the passageways.
That's what he wants us to believe. Look at this symbol that looks like an eye!
Don't you get it?
EEEEE
Remember that last sentence Grandpa Gabe wrote!
Take as much stuff as you can, and let's get out of here fast!
SPLURT
Aah!
KPLORTCH

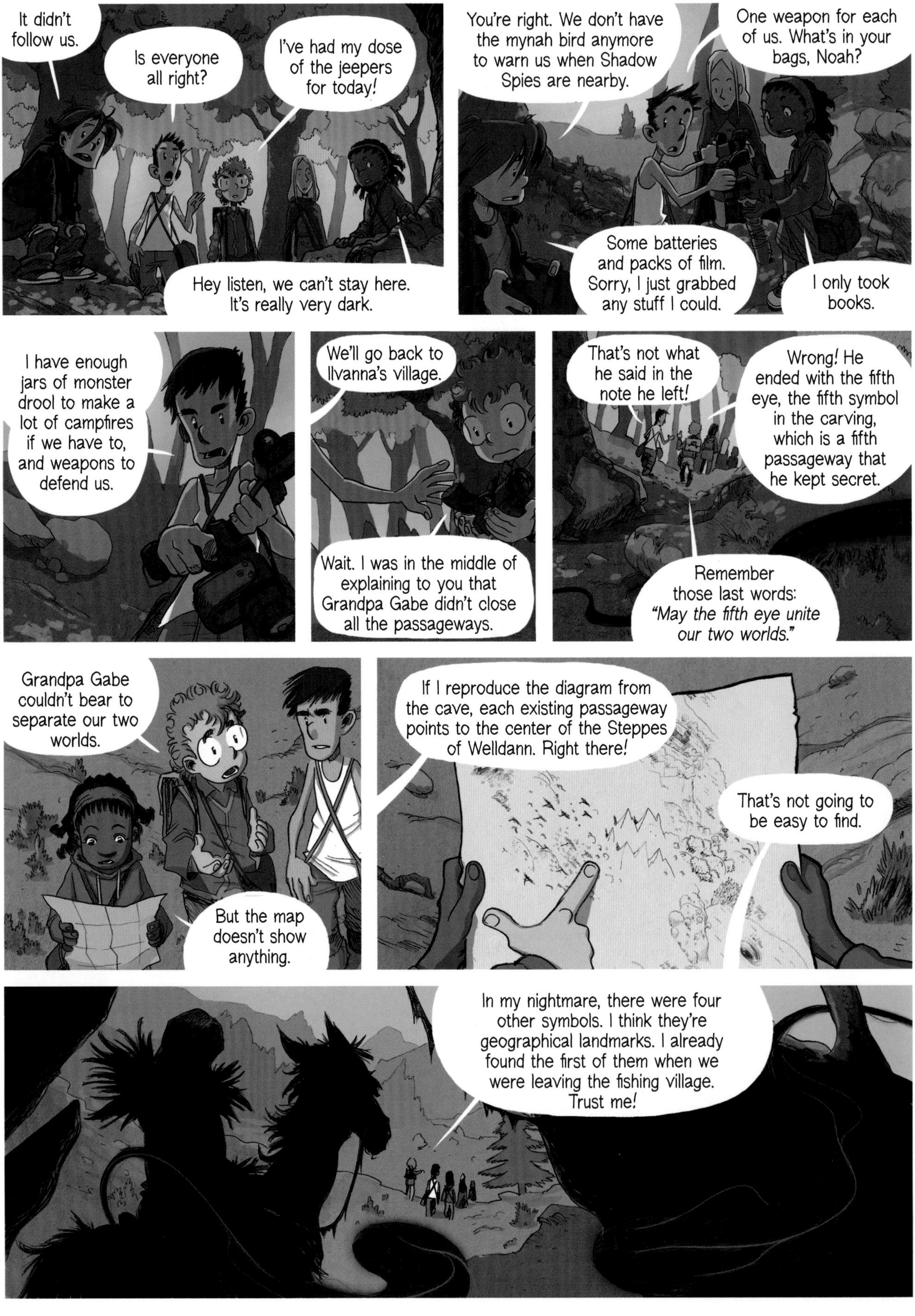
It didn't follow us.
Is everyone all right?
I've had my dose of the jeepers for today!
Hey listen, we can't stay here. It's really very dark.
You're right. We don't have the mynah bird anymore to warn us when Shadow Spies are nearby.
One weapon for each of us. What's in your bags, Noah?
Some batteries and packs of film. Sorry, I just grabbed any stuff I could.
I only took books.
I have enough jars of monster drool to make a lot of campfires if we have to, and weapons to defend us.
We'll go back to Ilvanna's village.
Wait. I was in the middle of explaining to you that Grandpa Gabe didn't close all the passageways.
That's not what he said in the note he left!
Wrong! He ended with the fifth eye, the fifth symbol in the carving, which is a fifth passageway that he kept secret.
Remember those last words: *"May the fifth eye unite our two worlds."*
Grandpa Gabe couldn't bear to separate our two worlds.
But the map doesn't show anything.
If I reproduce the diagram from the cave, each existing passageway points to the center of the Steppes of Welldann. Right there!
That's not going to be easy to find.
In my nightmare, there were four other symbols. I think they're geographical landmarks. I already found the first of them when we were leaving the fishing village. Trust me!

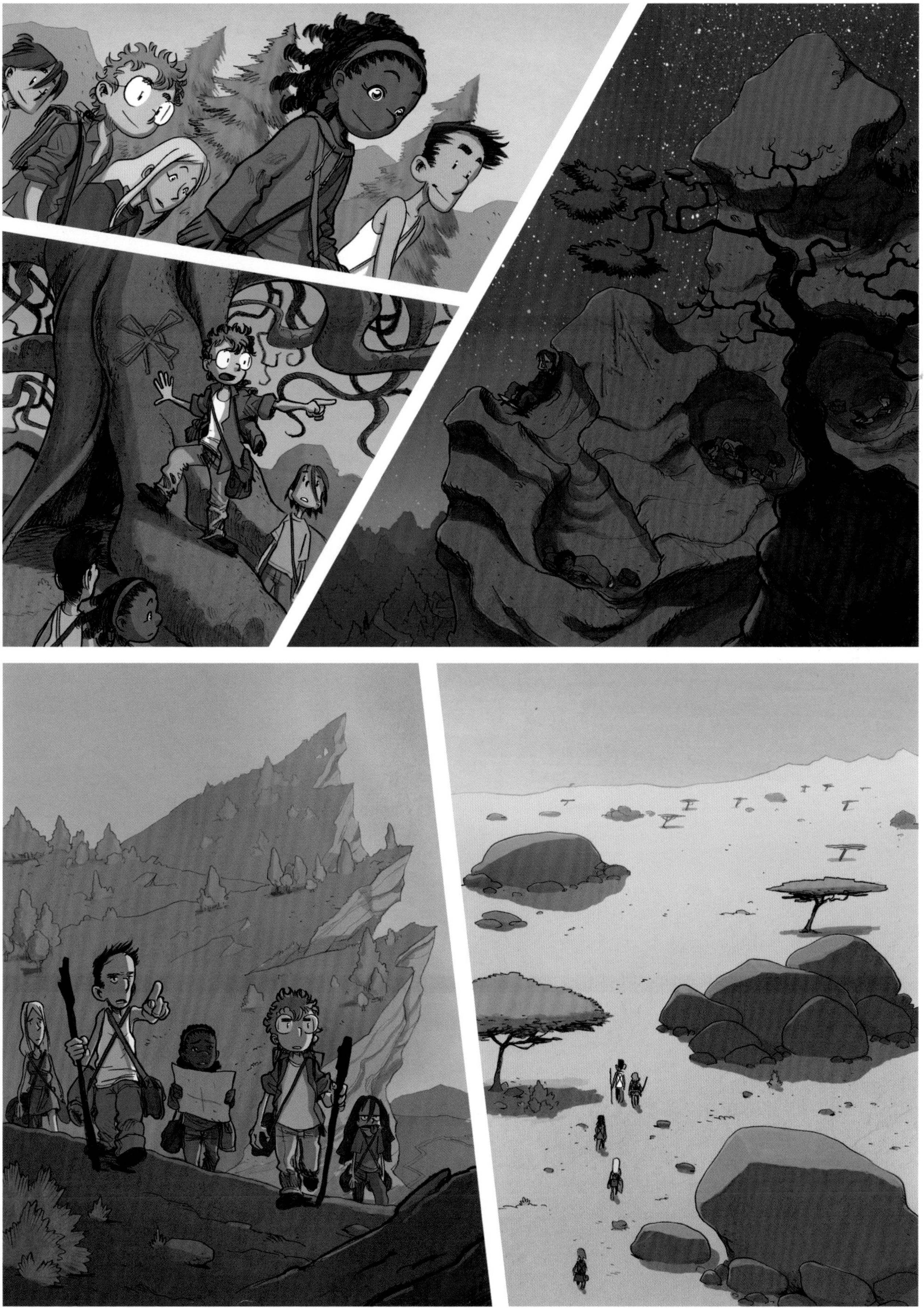

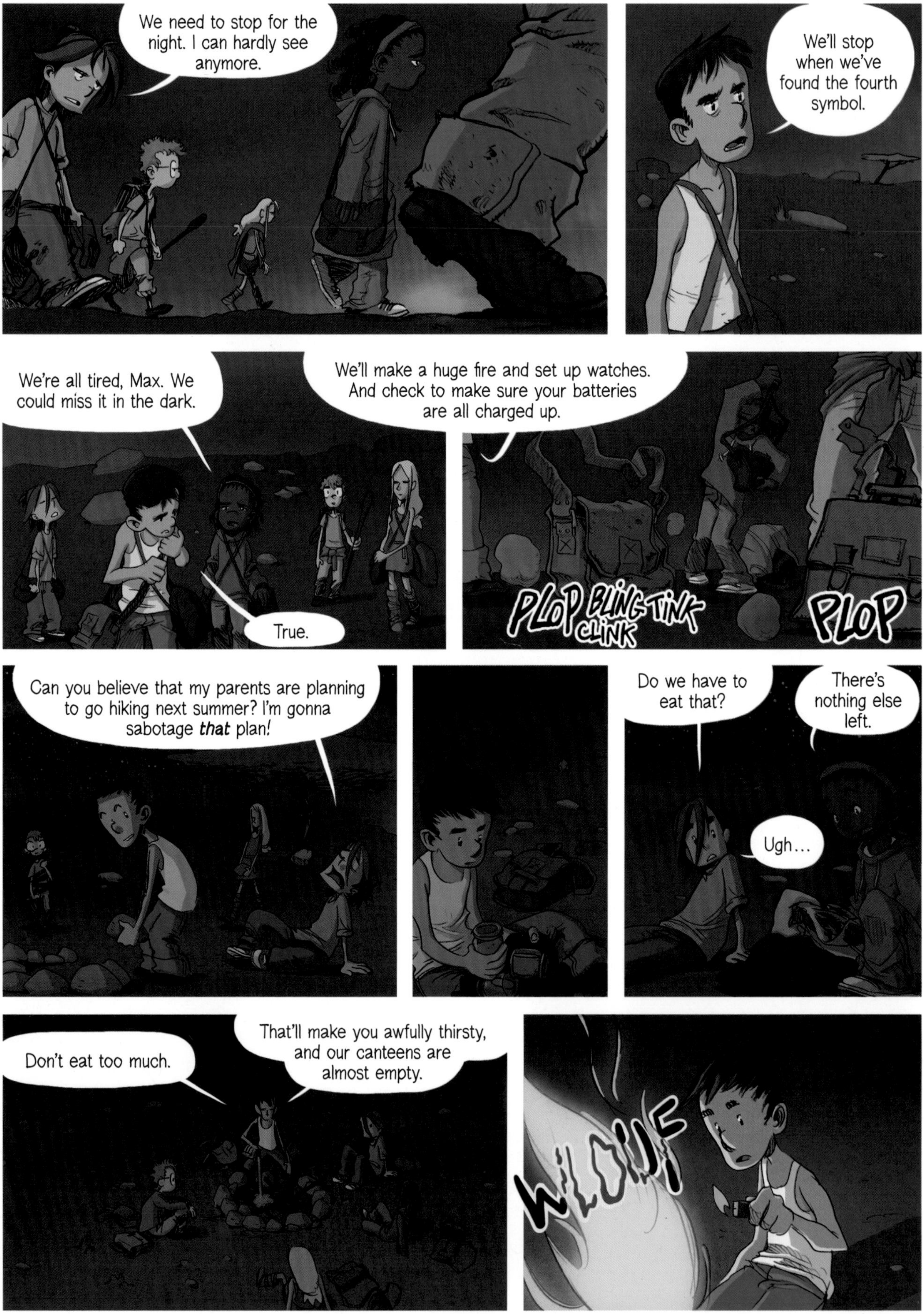
We need to stop for the night. I can hardly see anymore.
We'll stop when we've found the fourth symbol.
We're all tired, Max. We could miss it in the dark.
True.
We'll make a huge fire and set up watches. And check to make sure your batteries are all charged up.
PLOP BLING TINK CLINK
PLOP
Can you believe that my parents are planning to go hiking next summer? I'm gonna sabotage ***that*** plan!
Do we have to eat that?
There's nothing else left.
Ugh...
Don't eat too much.
That'll make you awfully thirsty, and our canteens are almost empty.
WLOUF

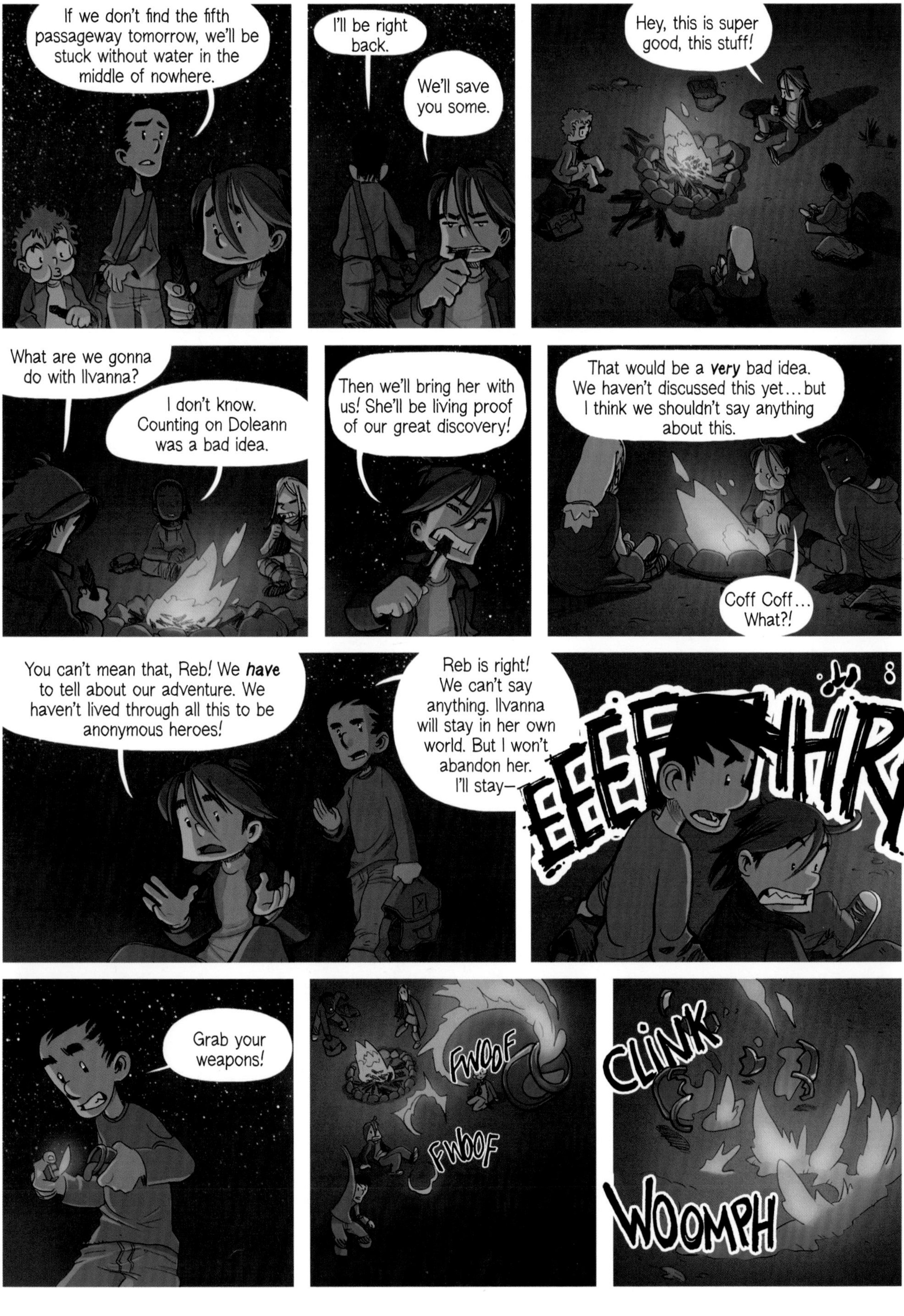
If we don't find the fifth passageway tomorrow, we'll be stuck without water in the middle of nowhere.
I'll be right back.
We'll save you some.
Hey, this is super good, this stuff!
What are we gonna do with Ilvanna?
I don't know. Counting on Doleann was a bad idea.
Then we'll bring her with us! She'll be living proof of our great discovery!
That would be a **very** bad idea. We haven't discussed this yet... but I think we shouldn't say anything about this.
Coff Coff... What?!
You can't mean that, Reb! We ***have*** to tell about our adventure. We haven't lived through all this to be anonymous heroes!
Reb is right! We can't say anything. Ilvanna will stay in her own world. But I won't abandon her. I'll stay—
EEEEEHHRR
Grab your weapons!
FWOOF
FWOOF
CLINK
WOOMPH

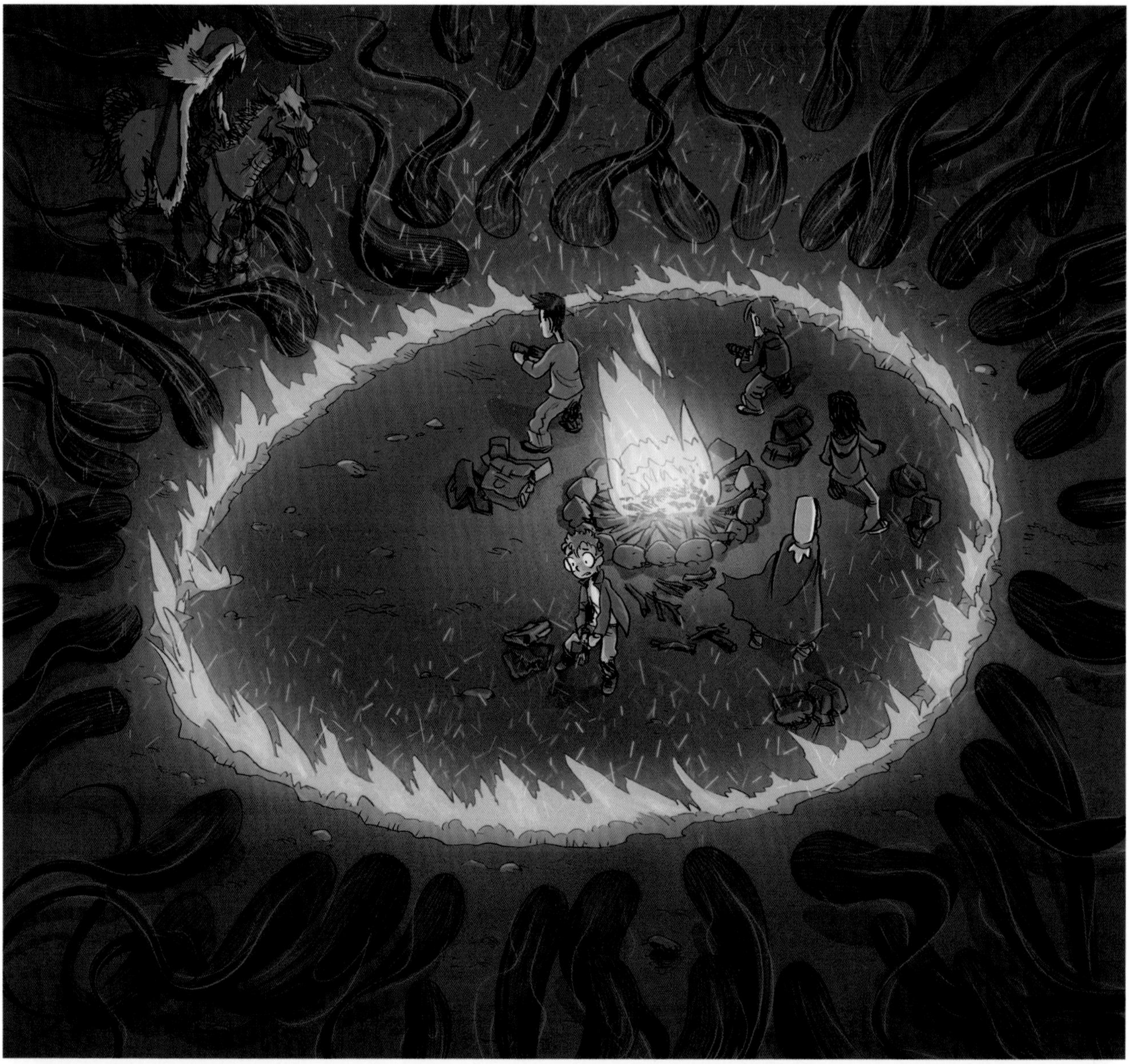

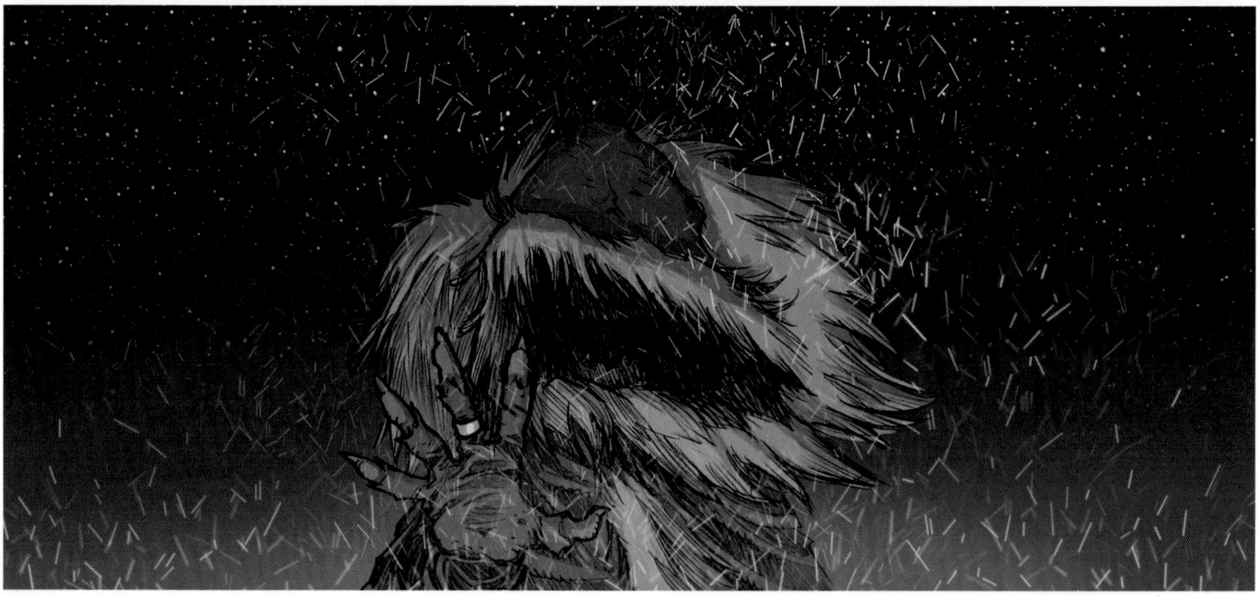

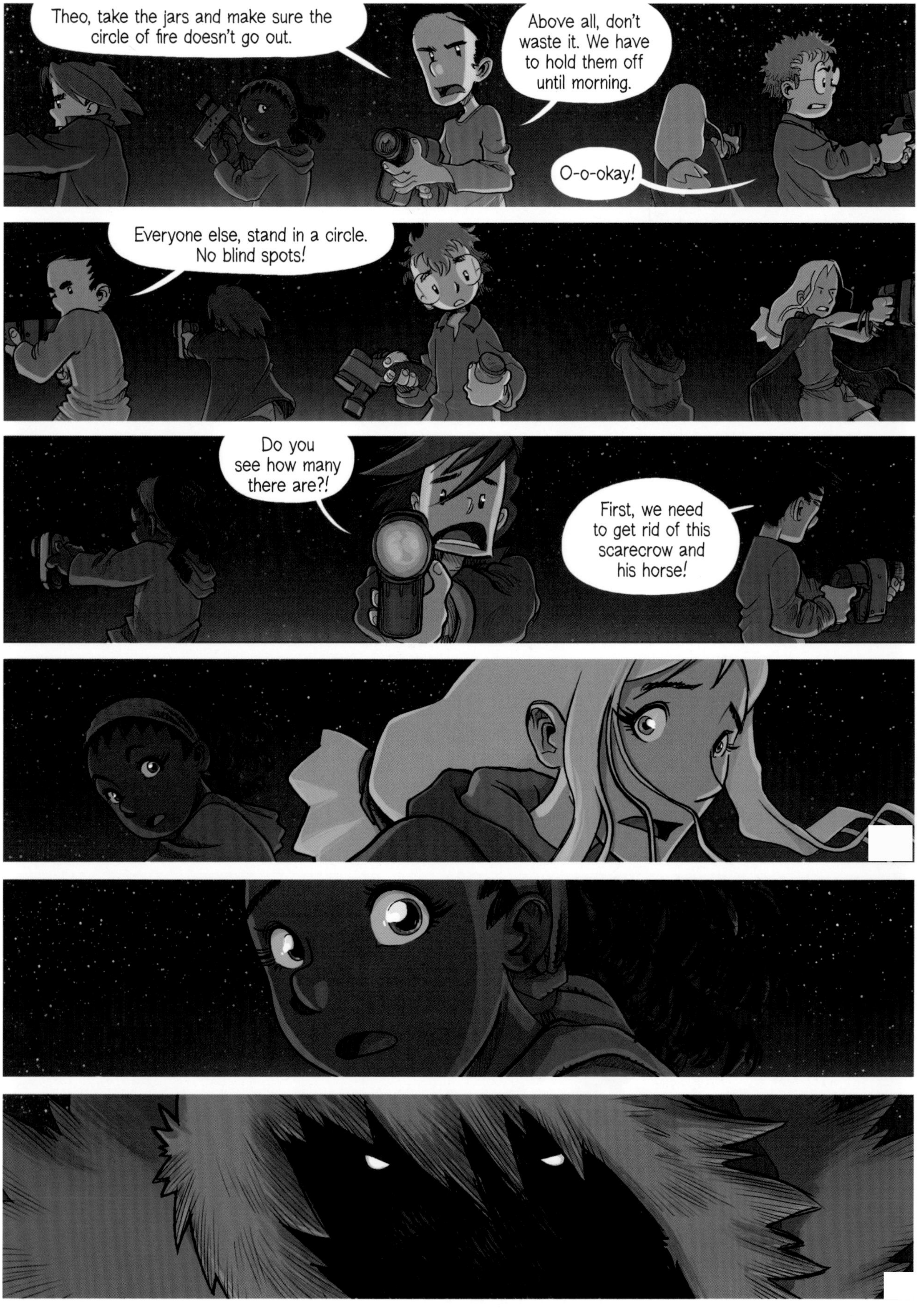
Theo, take the jars and make sure the circle of fire doesn't go out.
Above all, don't waste it. We have to hold them off until morning.
O-o-okay!
Everyone else, stand in a circle. No blind spots!
Do you see how many there are?!
First, we need to get rid of this scarecrow and his horse!

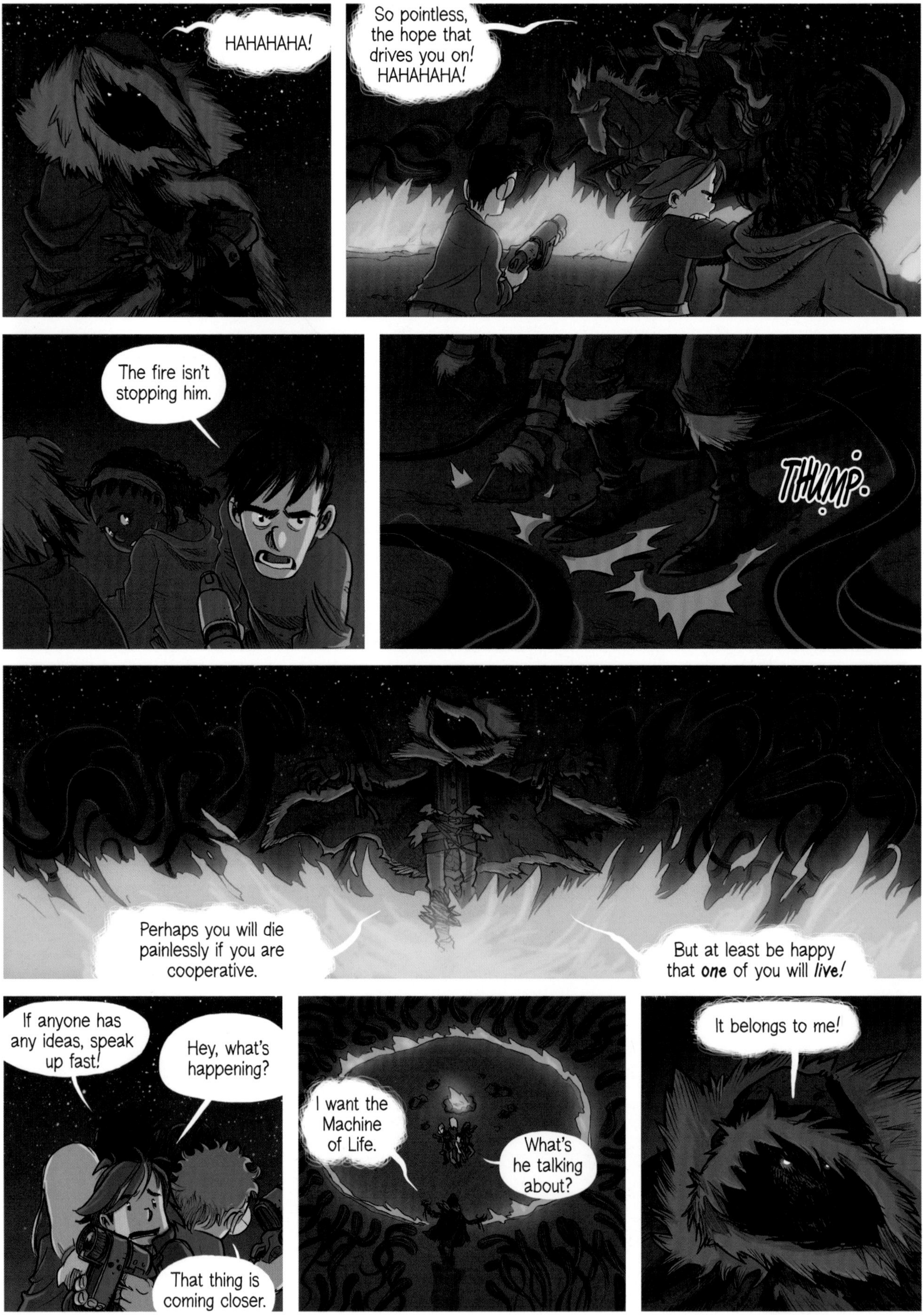
HAHAHAHA!
So pointless, the hope that drives you on! HAHAHAHA!
The fire isn't stopping him.
THUMP.
Perhaps you will die painlessly if you are cooperative.
But at least be happy that *one* of you will *live!*
If anyone has any ideas, speak up fast!
Hey, what's happening?
That thing is coming closer.
I want the Machine of Life.
What's he talking about?
It belongs to me!

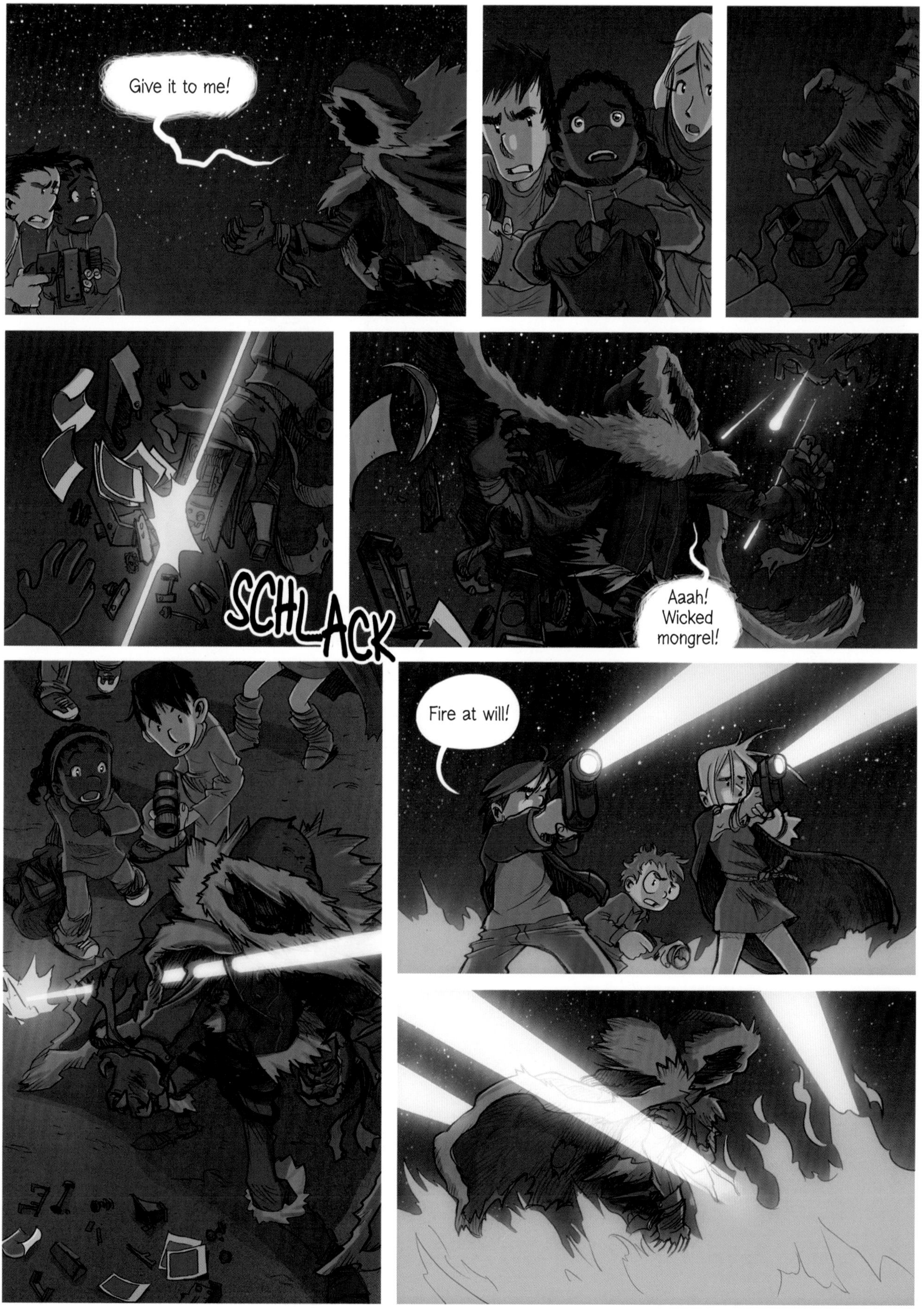
Give it to me!
SCHLACK
Aaah! Wicked mongrel!
Fire at will!

EEEEEEHH

All right!

EEEEEEEEHHHH

There... it's a sign.

Este Doleann!

All right! We can't let her do all the work!

We're saved!

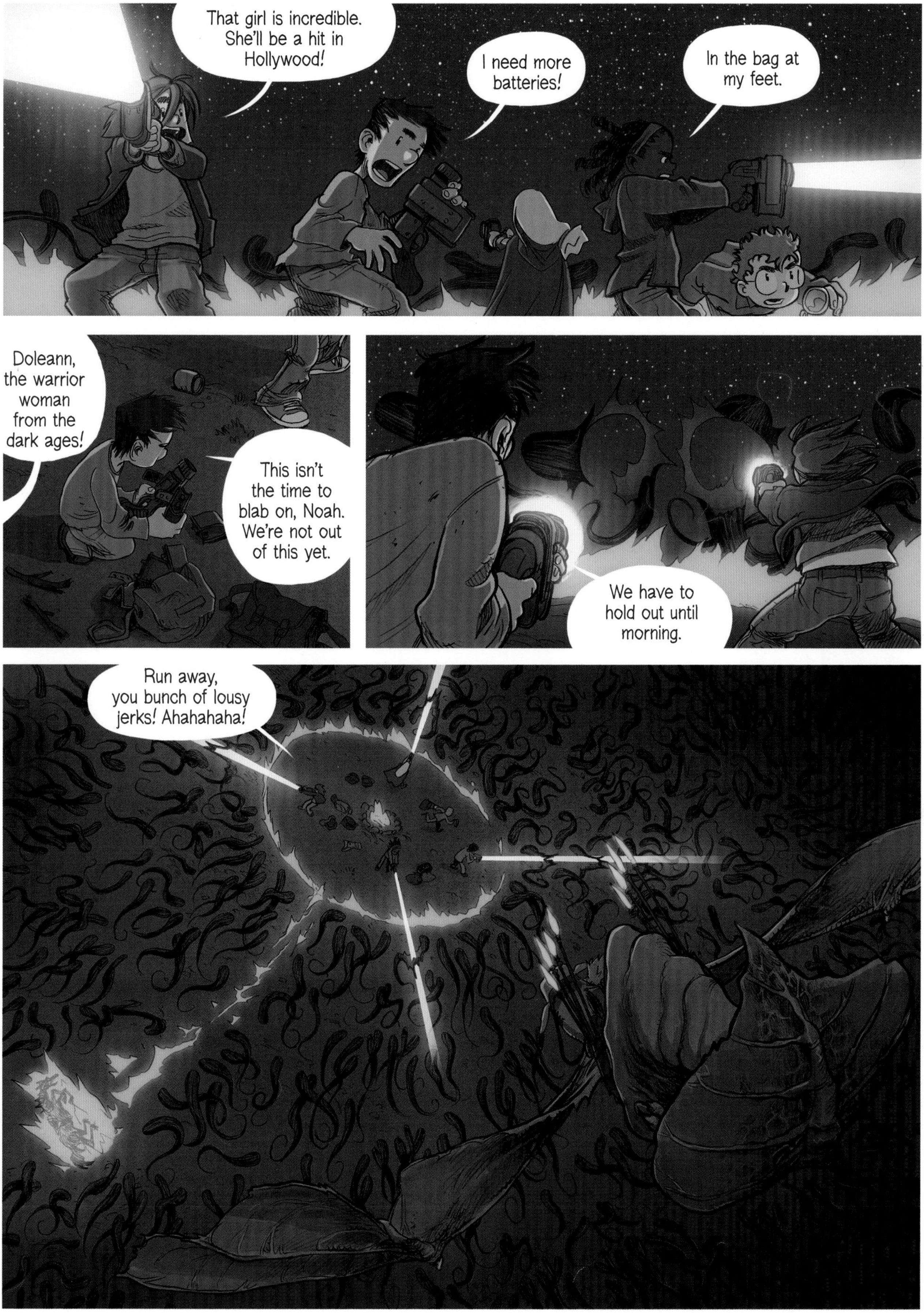
That girl is incredible. She'll be a hit in Hollywood!
I need more batteries!
In the bag at my feet.
Doleann, the warrior woman from the dark ages!
This isn't the time to blab on, Noah. We're not out of this yet.
We have to hold out until morning.
Run away, you bunch of lousy jerks! Ahahahaha!

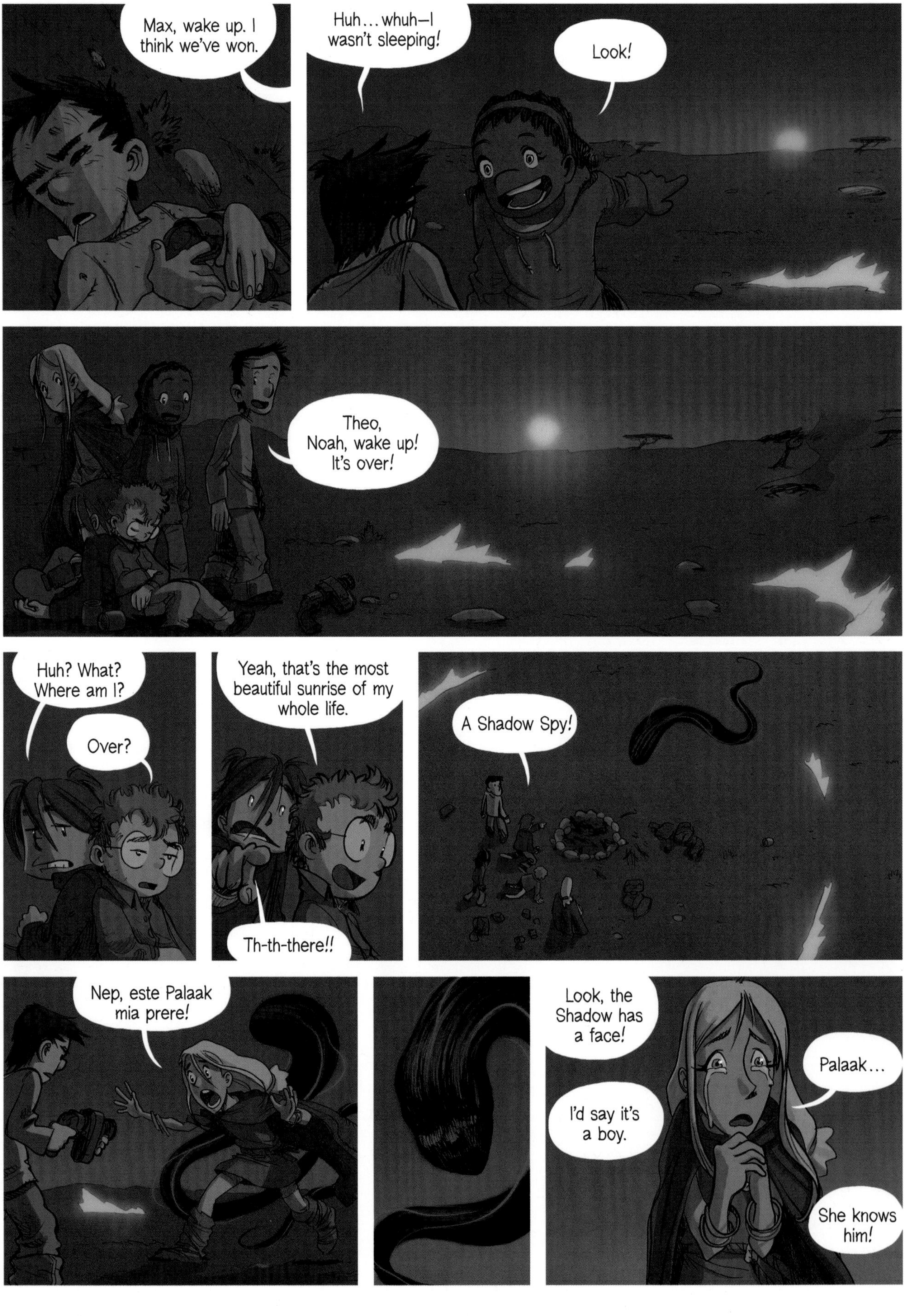
Max, wake up. I think we've won.
Huh... whuh—I wasn't sleeping!
Look!
Theo, Noah, wake up! It's over!
Huh? What? Where am I?
Over?
Yeah, that's the most beautiful sunrise of my whole life.
Th-th-there!!
A Shadow Spy!
Nep, este Palaak mia prere!
Look, the Shadow has a face!
I'd say it's a boy.
Palaak...
She knows him!

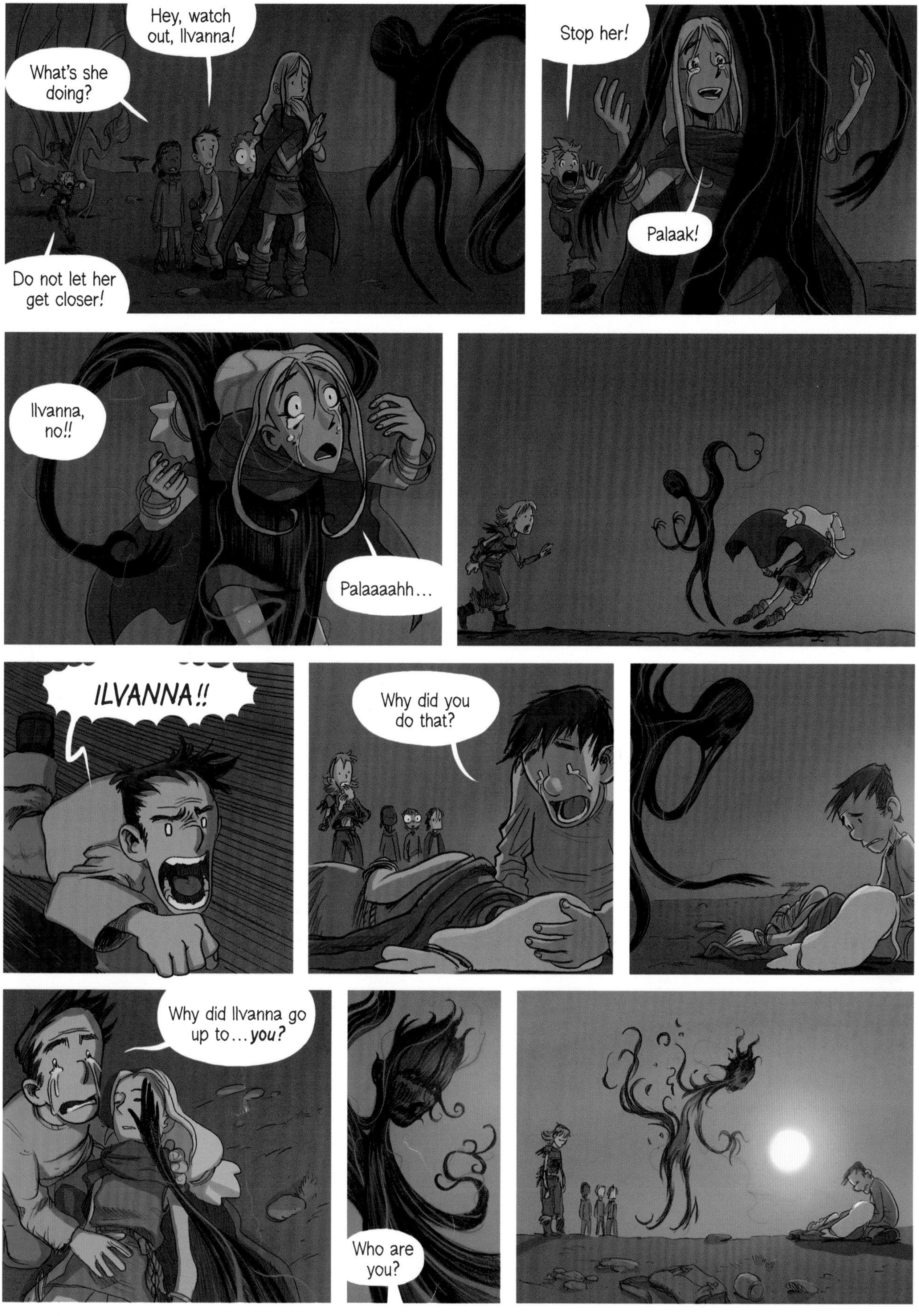
What's she doing?
Hey, watch out, Ilvanna!
Do not let her get closer!
Stop her!
Palaak!
Ilvanna, no!!
Palaaaahh…
ILVANNA!!
Why did you do that?
Why did Ilvanna go up to… *you?*
Who are you?

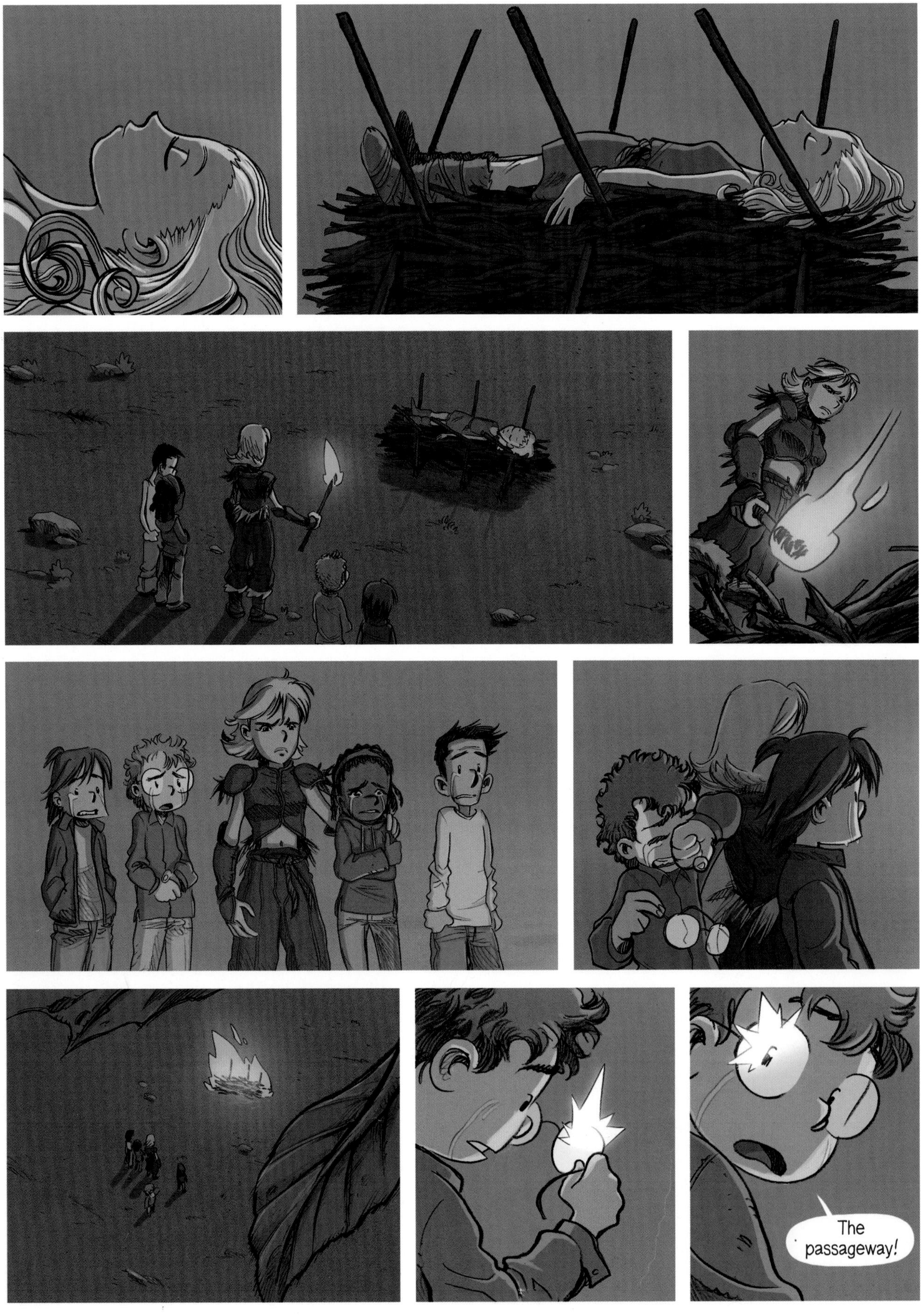
The passageway!

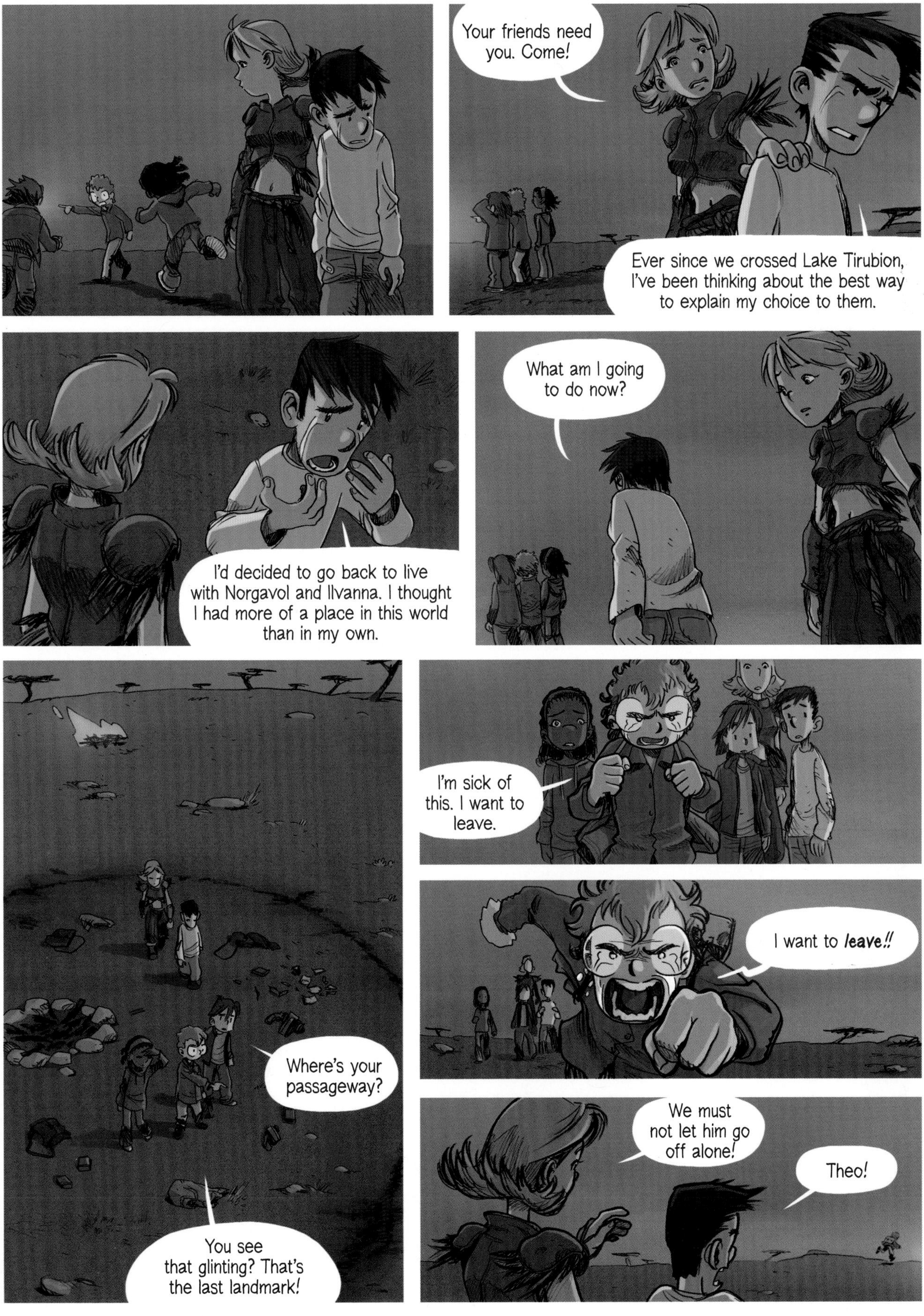
Your friends need you. Come!
Ever since we crossed Lake Tirubion, I've been thinking about the best way to explain my choice to them.
I'd decided to go back to live with Norgavol and Ilvanna. I thought I had more of a place in this world than in my own.
What am I going to do now?
Where's your passageway?
You see that glinting? That's the last landmark!
I'm sick of this. I want to leave.
I want to ***leave!!***
We must not let him go off alone!
Theo!

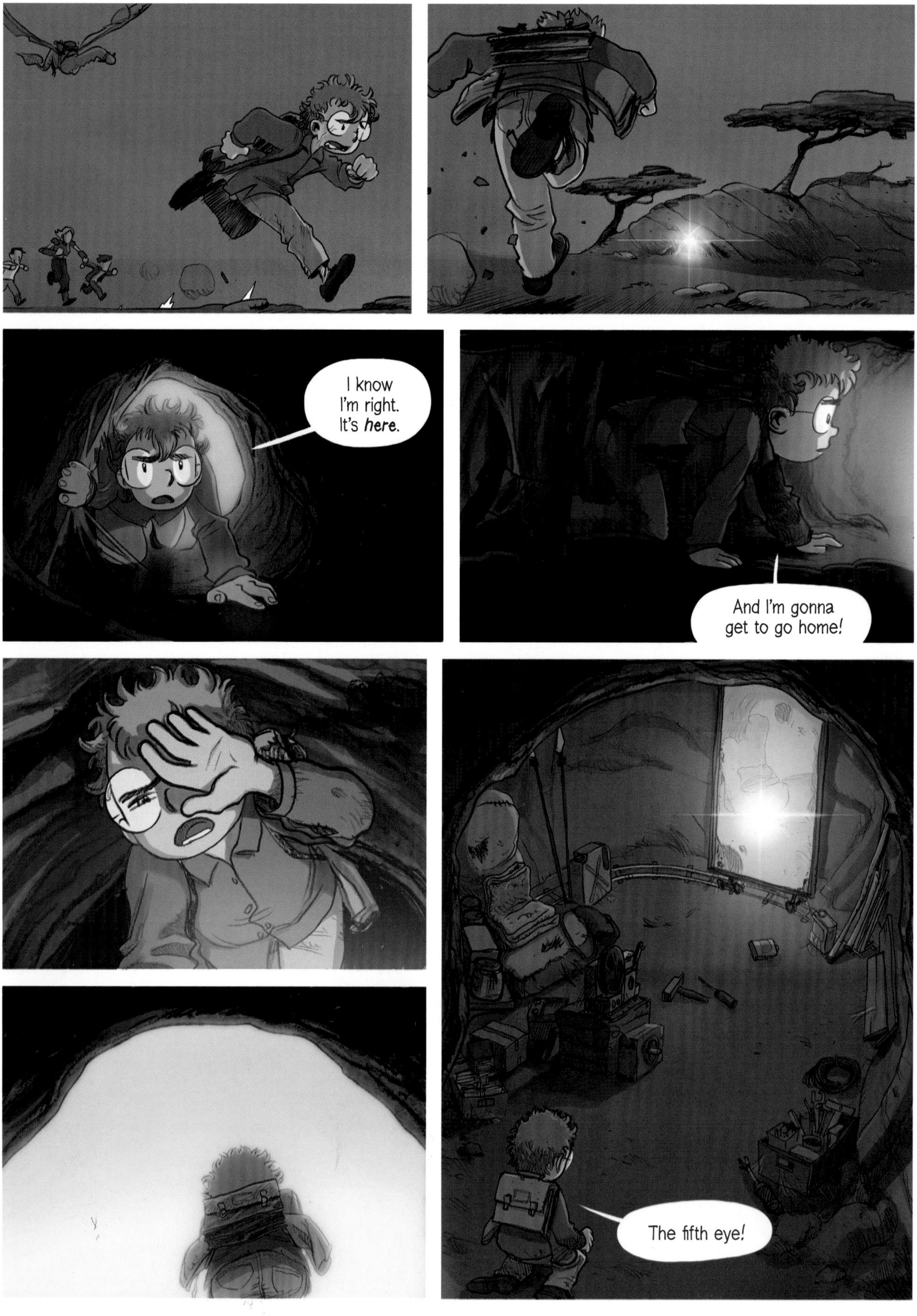
I know
I'm right.
It's *here*.
And I'm gonna
get to go home!
The fifth eye!

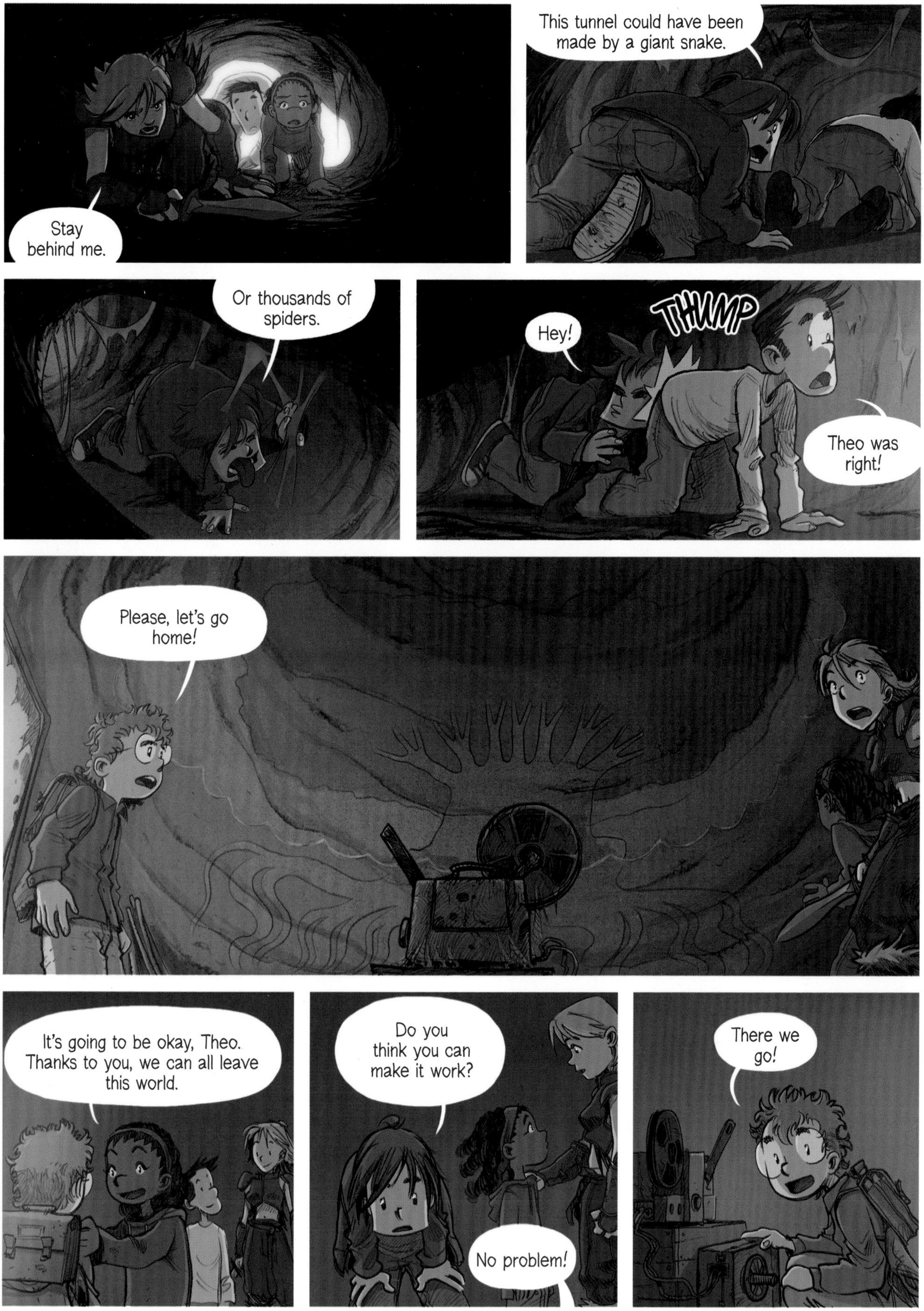
Stay behind me.
This tunnel could have been made by a giant snake.
Or thousands of spiders.
Hey!
THUMP
Theo was right!
Please, let's go home!
It's going to be okay, Theo. Thanks to you, we can all leave this world.
Do you think you can make it work?
No problem!
There we go!

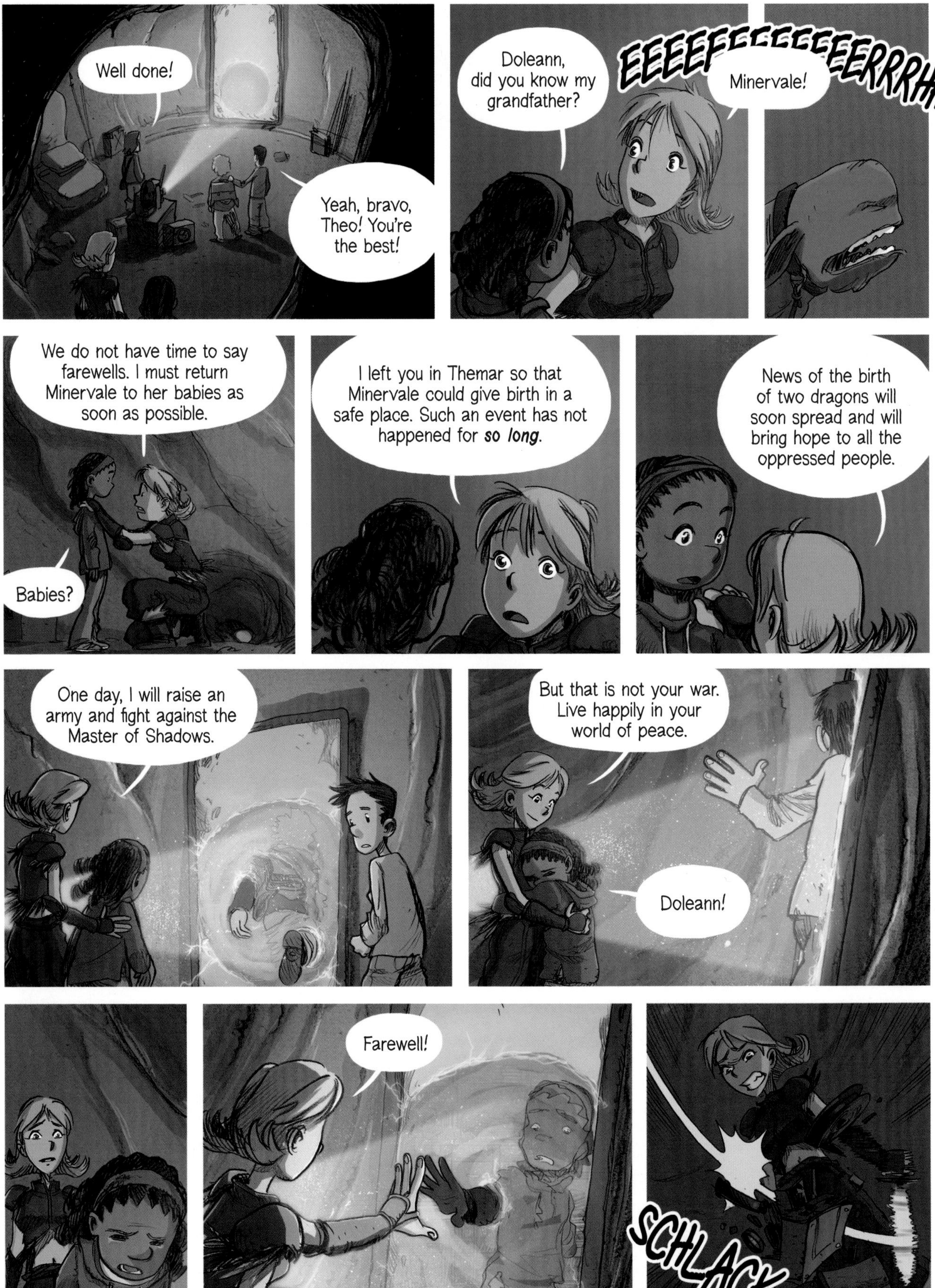

Well done!
Yeah, bravo, Theo! You're the best!
Doleann, did you know my grandfather?
Minervale!
EEEEFFFFFFFFFEERRRHH
We do not have time to say farewells. I must return Minervale to her babies as soon as possible.
Babies?
I left you in Themar so that Minervale could give birth in a safe place. Such an event has not happened for **so *long***.
News of the birth of two dragons will soon spread and will bring hope to all the oppressed people.
One day, I will raise an army and fight against the Master of Shadows.
But that is not your war. Live happily in your world of peace.
Doleann!
Farewell!
SCHLACK

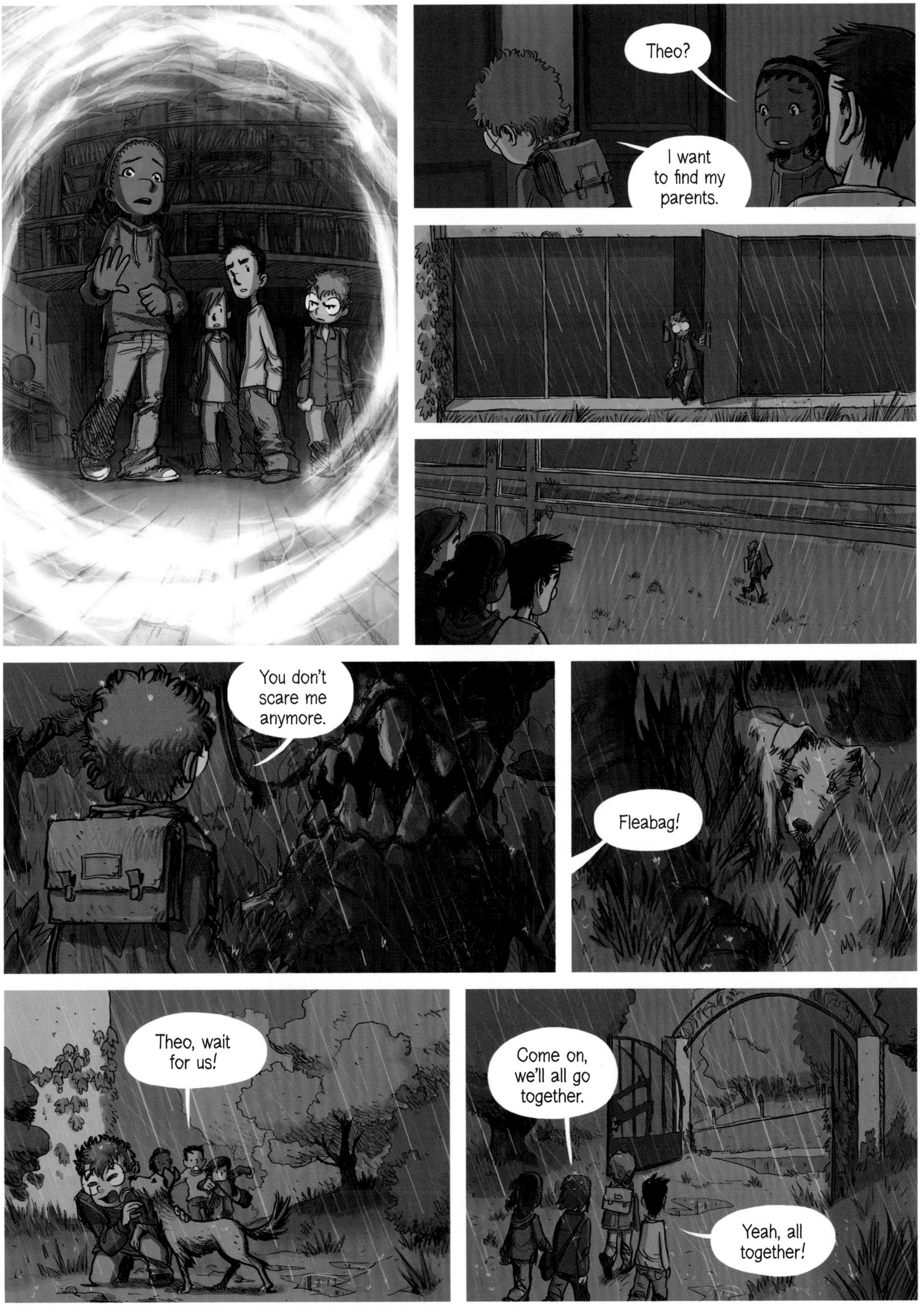
Theo?
I want to find my parents.
You don't scare me anymore.
Fleabag!
Theo, wait for us!
Come on, we'll all go together.
Yeah, all together!

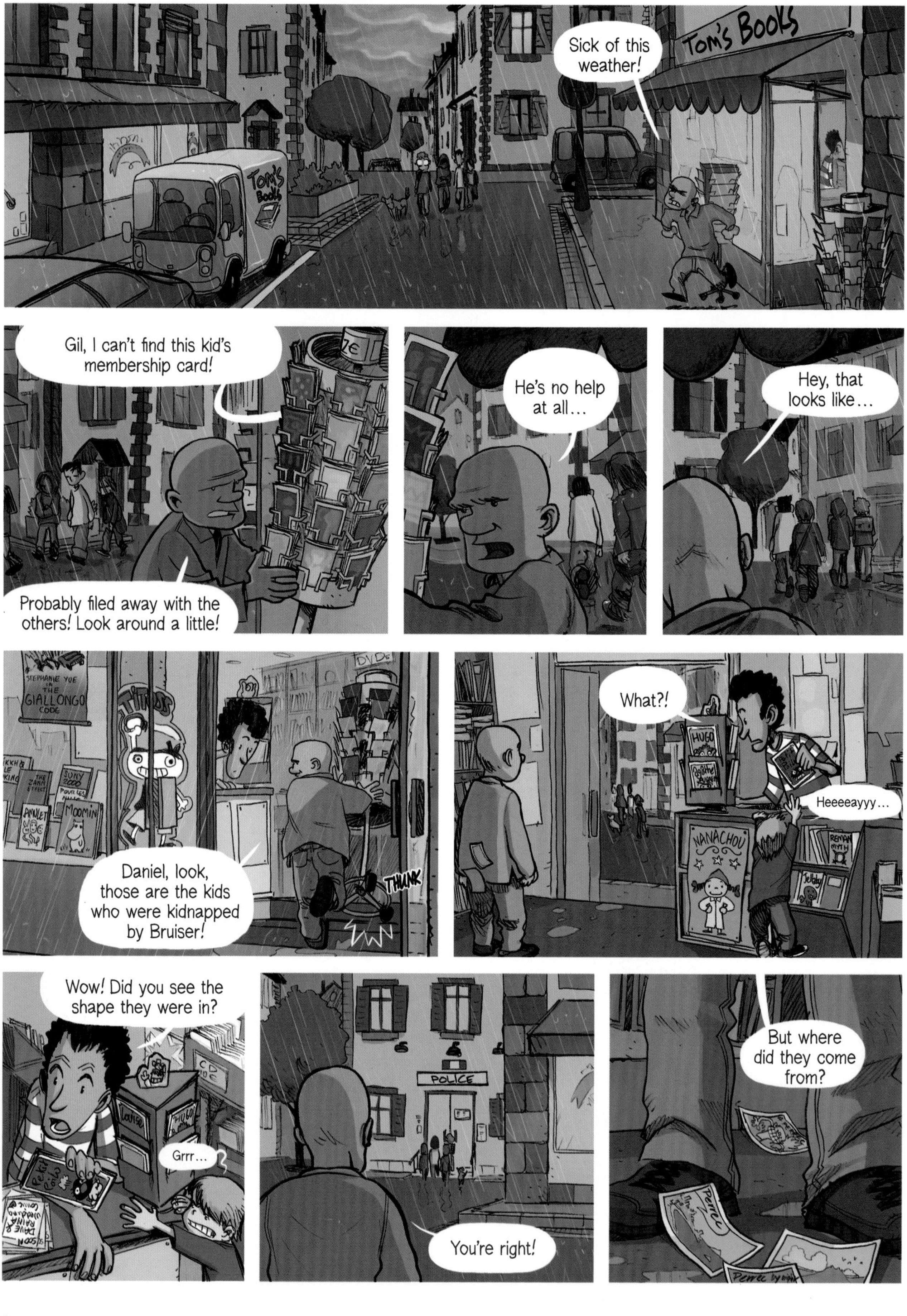
Tom's Books
Sick of this weather!
Tom's Books
Gil, I can't find this kid's membership card!
Probably filed away with the others! Look around a little!
He's no help at all...
Hey, that looks like...
Daniel, look, those are the kids who were kidnapped by Bruiser!
THUNK
What?!
Heeeeayyy...
Wow! Did you see the shape they were in?
Grrr...
POLICE
You're right!
But where did they come from?

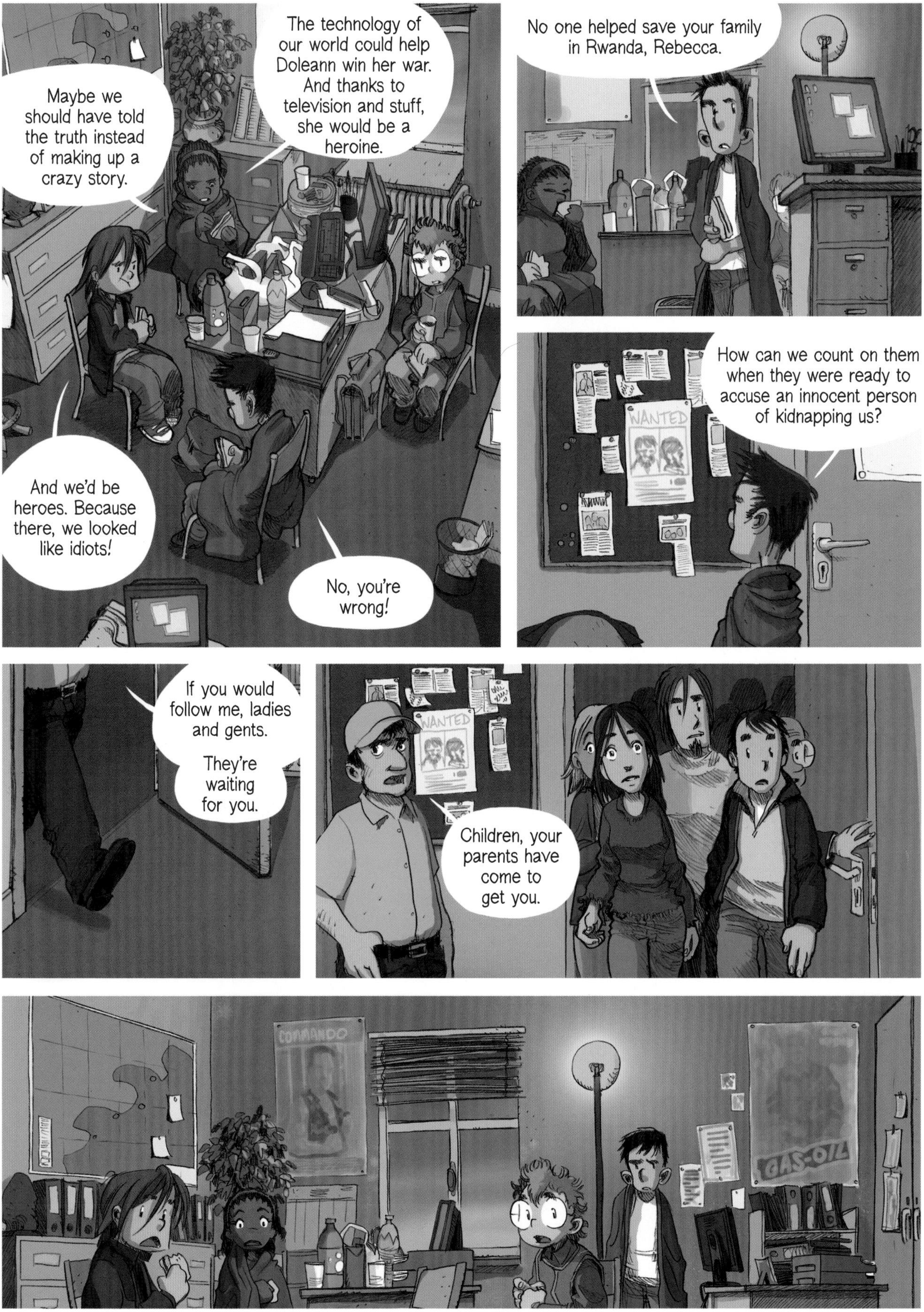
Maybe we should have told the truth instead of making up a crazy story.
The technology of our world could help Doleann win her war. And thanks to television and stuff, she would be a heroine.
And we'd be heroes. Because there, we looked like idiots!
No, you're wrong!
No one helped save your family in Rwanda, Rebecca.
How can we count on them when they were ready to accuse an innocent person of kidnapping us?
WANTED
If you would follow me, ladies and gents.
They're waiting for you.
WANTED
Children, your parents have come to get you.
COMMANDO
GAS-OIL

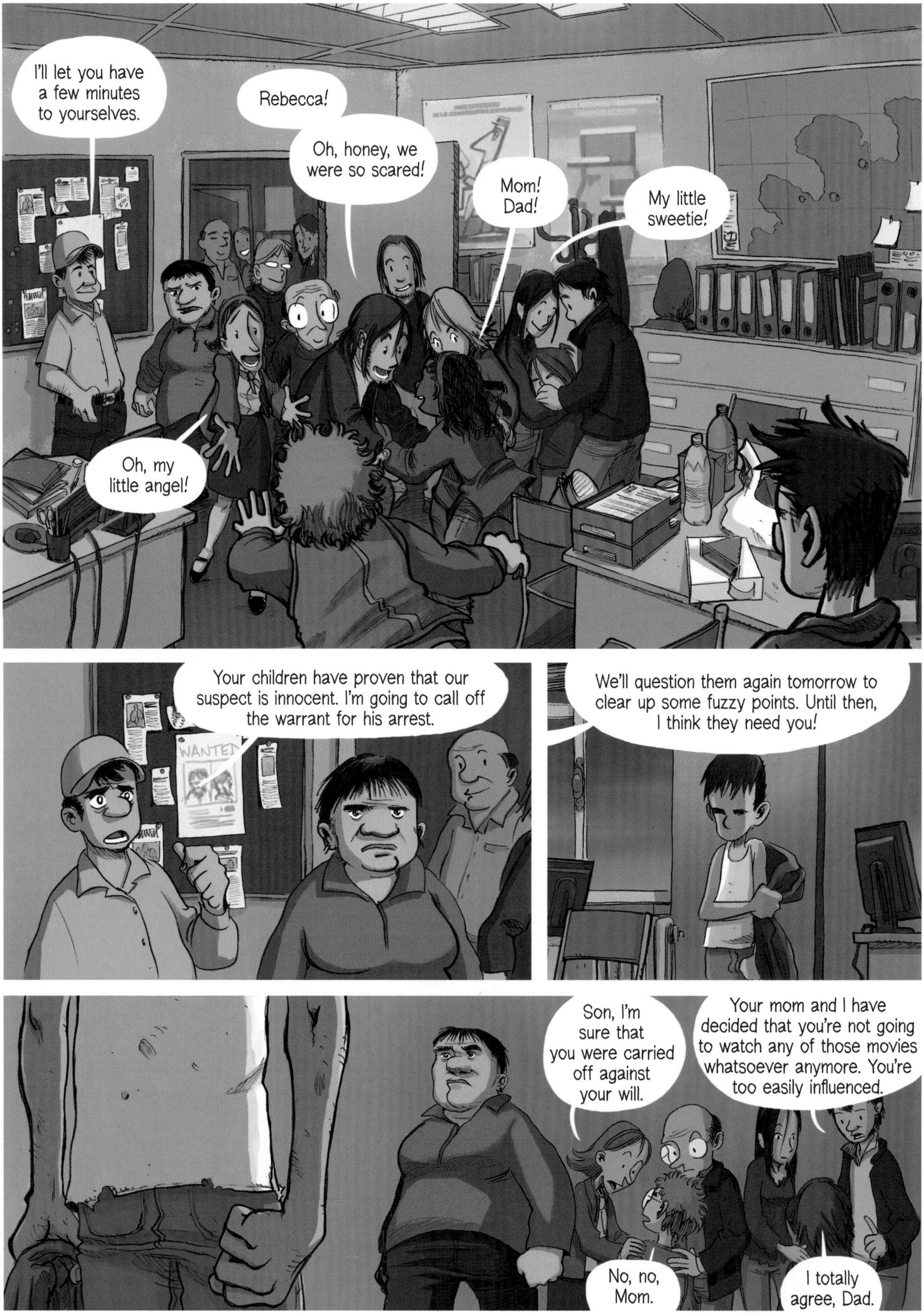
I'll let you have a few minutes to yourselves.
Rebecca!
Oh, honey, we were so scared!
Mom! Dad!
My little sweetie!
Oh, my little angel!
Your children have proven that our suspect is innocent. I'm going to call off the warrant for his arrest.
WANTED
We'll question them again tomorrow to clear up some fuzzy points. Until then, I think they need you!
Son, I'm sure that you were carried off against your will.
No, no, Mom.
Your mom and I have decided that you're not going to watch any of those movies whatsoever anymore. You're too easily influenced.
I totally agree, Dad.

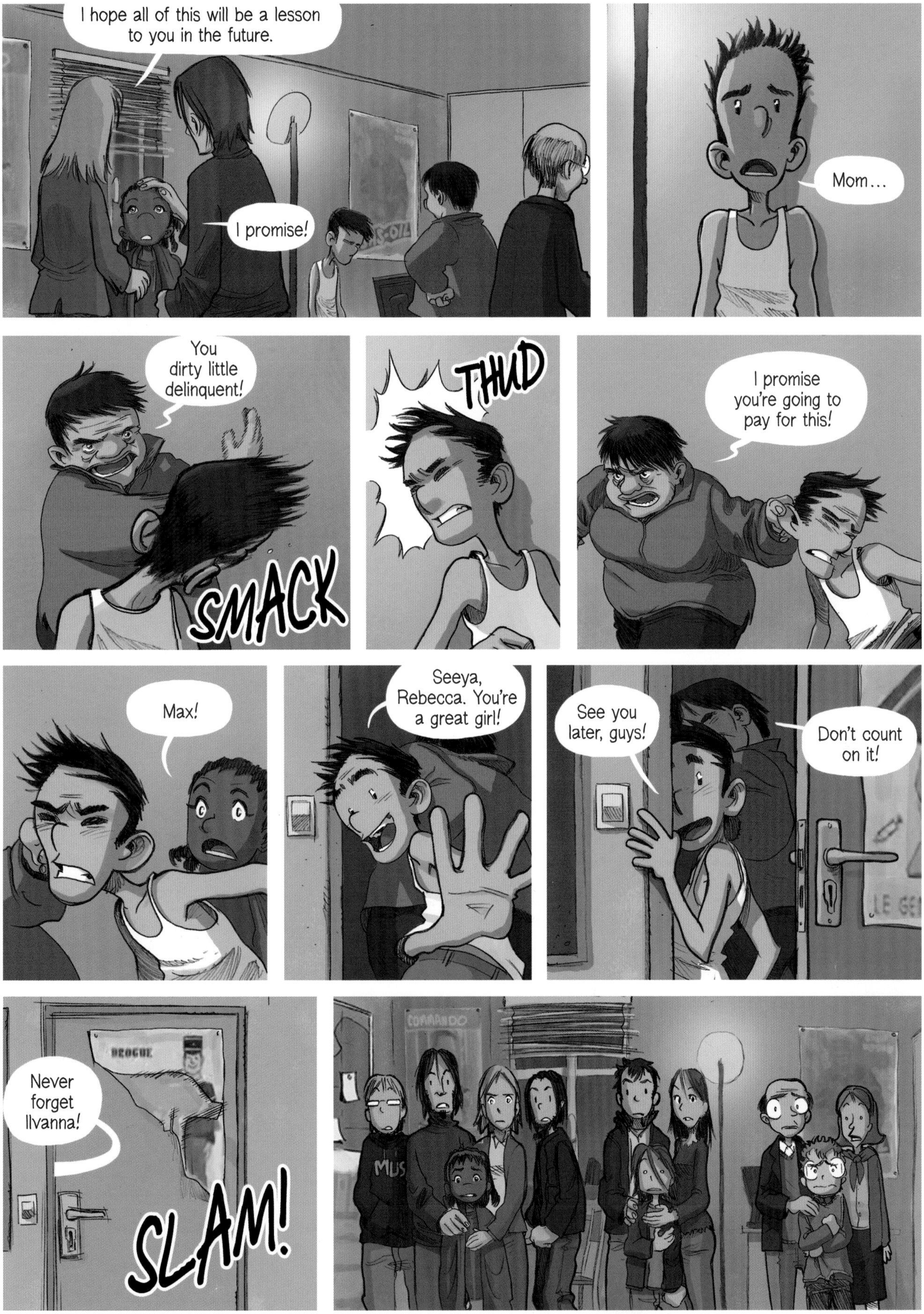
I hope all of this will be a lesson to you in the future.
I promise!
Mom...
You dirty little delinquent!
SMACK
THUD
I promise you're going to pay for this!
Max!
Seeya, Rebecca. You're a great girl!
See you later, guys!
Don't count on it!
Never forget Ilvanna!
SLAM!

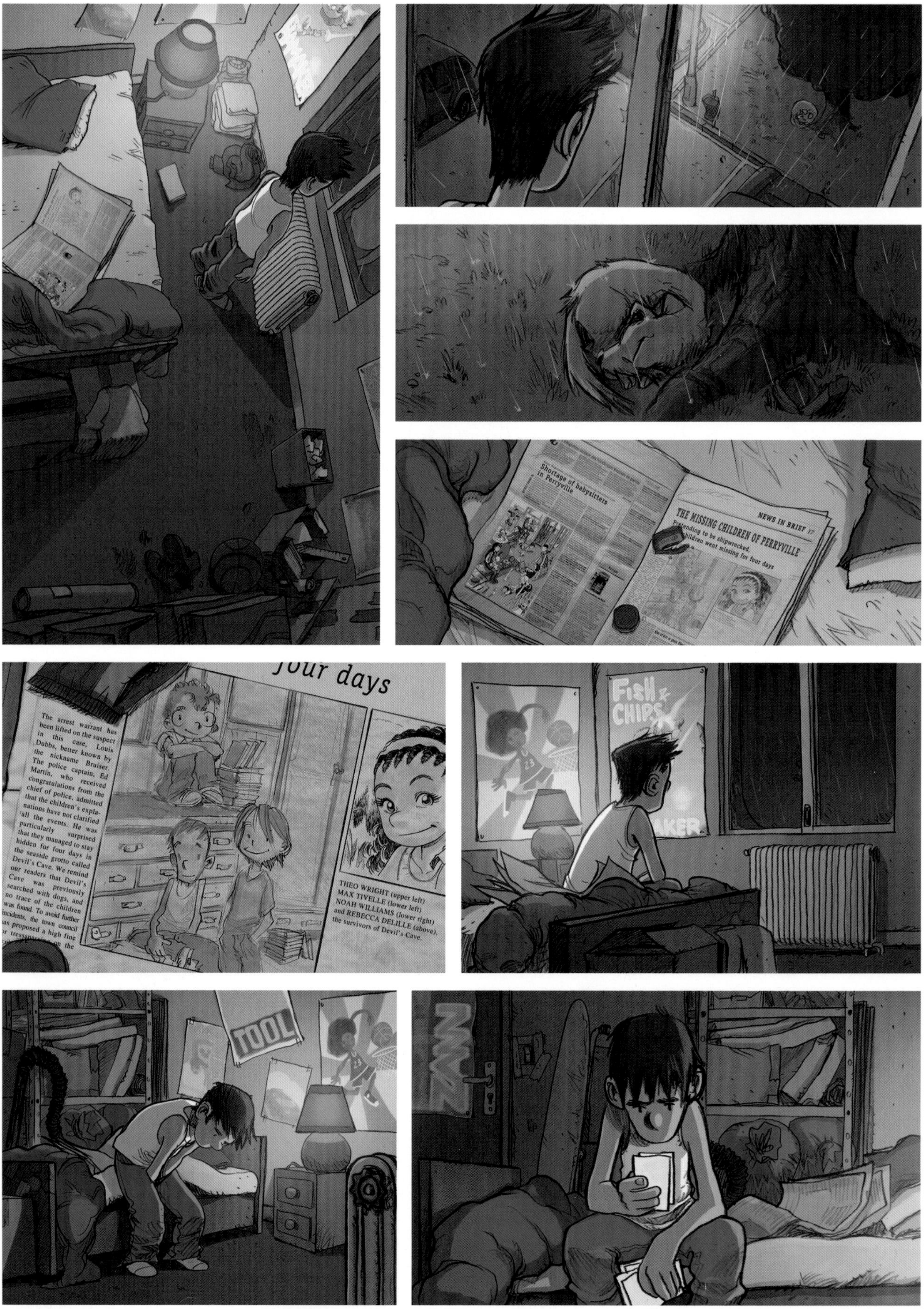
Shortage of babysitters in Perryville
NEWS IN BRIEF 17
THE MISSING CHILDREN OF PERRYVILLE
Pretending to be shipwrecked,
children went missing for four days
four days
The arrest warrant has been lifted on the suspect in this case, Louis Dubbs, better known by the nickname Bruiser. The police captain, Ed Martin, who received congratulations from the chief of police, admitted that the children's explanations have not clarified all the events. He was particularly surprised that they managed to stay hidden for four days in the seaside grotto called Devil's Cave. We remind our readers that Devil's Cave was previously searched with dogs, and no trace of the children was found. To avoid further incidents, the town council has proposed a high fine
THEO WRIGHT (upper left)
MAX TIVELLE (lower left)
NOAH WILLIAMS (lower right)
and REBECCA DELILLE (above),
the survivors of Devil's Cave.
FISH & CHIPS
AKER
TOOL

It can't end like this!

I have to go back.

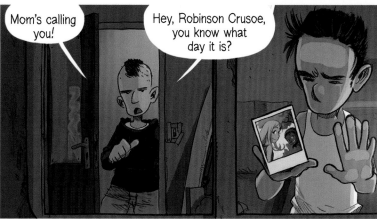

Mom's calling you!

Hey, Robinson Crusoe, you know what day it is?

Friday! Hahaha...

I'm going back.

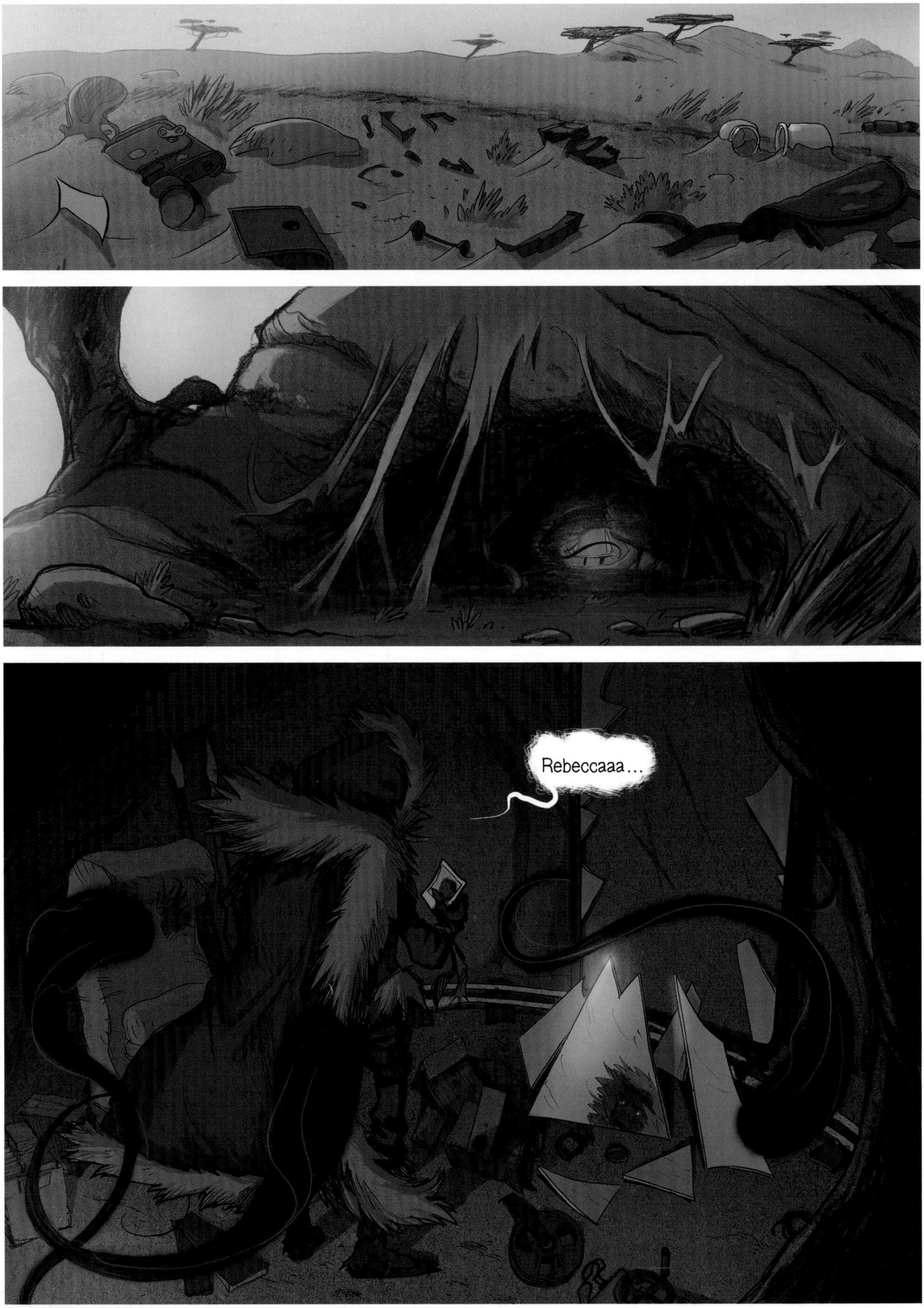
Rebeccaaa...

The End...?

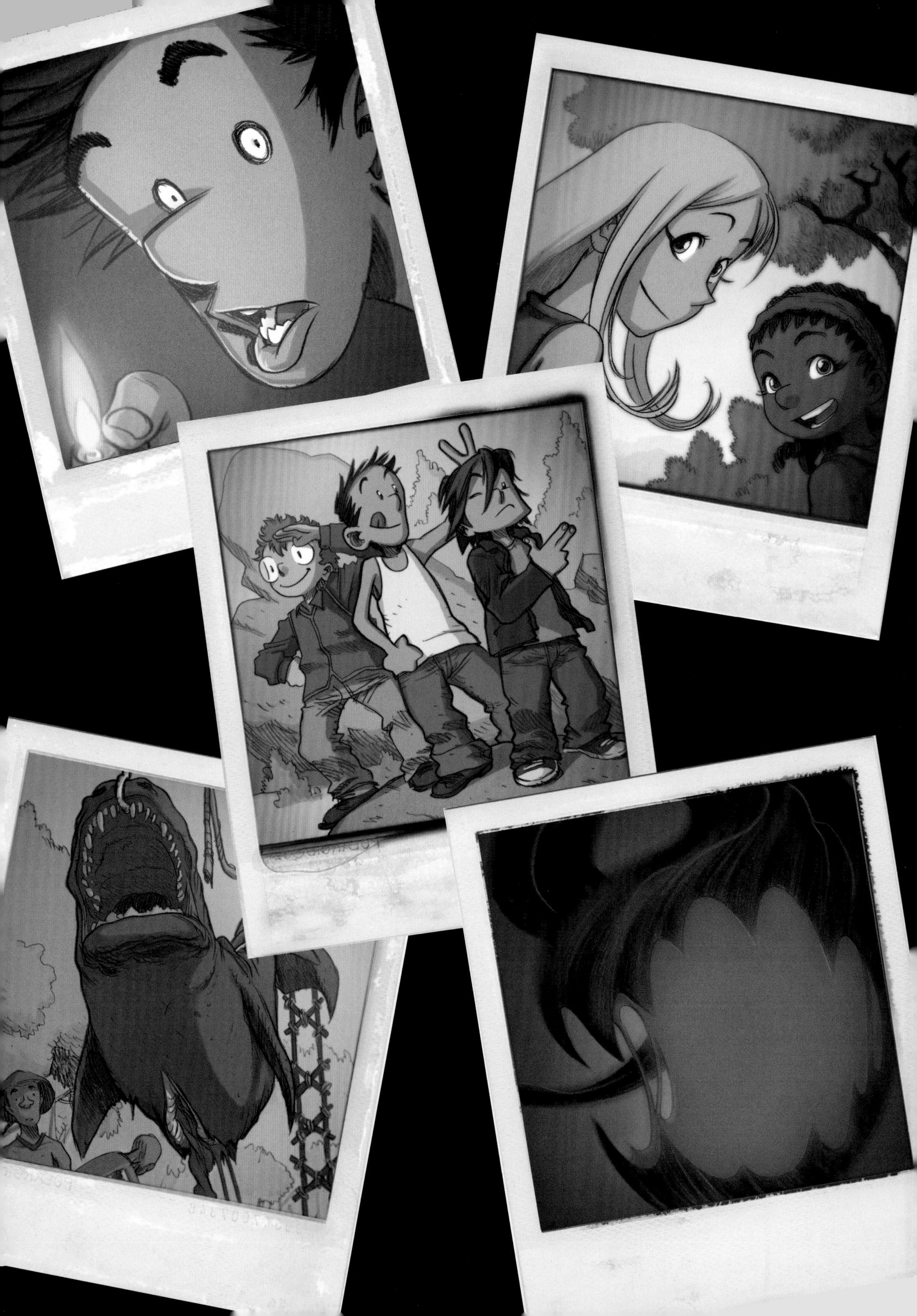

Art by Bannister
Story by Nykko
Colors by Jaffré
Translation by Carol Klio Burrell

First American edition published in 2009 by Graphic Universe™.
Published by arrangement with S.A. DUPUIS, Belgium.

Graphic Universe™
A division of Lerner Publishing Group, Inc.
241 First Avenue North
Minneapolis, MN 55401 U.S.A.

Website address: www.lernerbooks.com

Library of Congress Cataloging-in-Publication Data

Bannister. [Passage. English]
[Maître des ombres. English]
The Master of Shadows / art by Bannister ; story by Nykko ; [colors by Jaffré ;
translation by Carol Klio Burrell]. — 1st American ed.
p.   cm. — (The ElseWhere chronicles ; bk. 3)
Summary: After discovering that Grandpa Gabe has sealed the passageways between
worlds, Max, Rebecca, Theo, and Noah must confront the Master of Shadows himself
to find another way home.
ISBN: 978-0-7613-4461-2 (lib. bdg. : alk. paper)
1. Graphic novels. [1. Graphic novels. 2. Horror stories.] I. Nykko. II. Jaffré. III.
Burrell, Carol Klio. IV. Title.
PZ7.7.B34Mas 2009
741.5'973—dc22   2008039444

Manufactured in the United States of America
1 2 3 4 5 6 - BP - 14 13 12 11 10 09

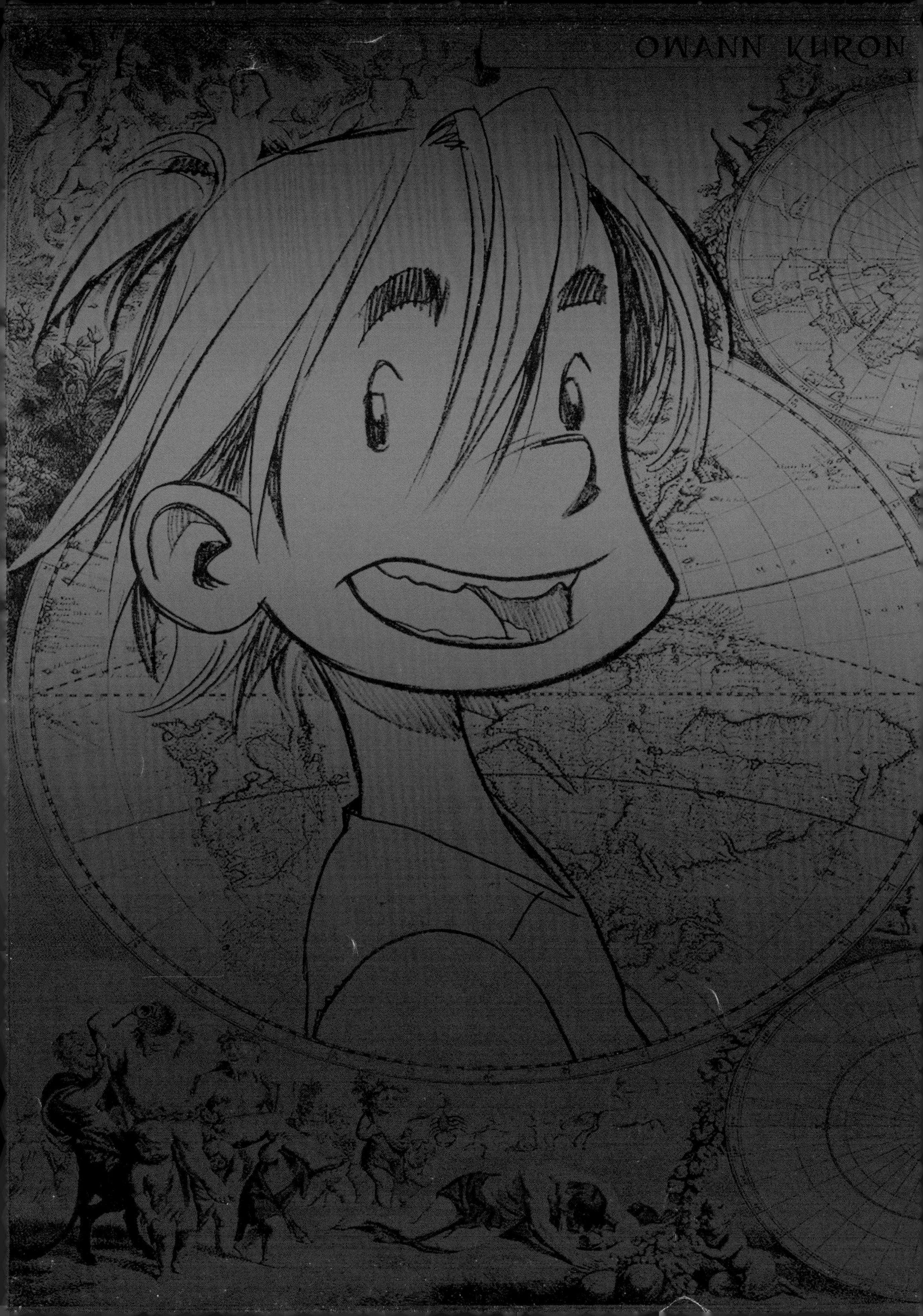
OWANN KURON